Amy Cross is the author of more than 250 horror,
paranormal, fantasy and thriller novels.

MAN ON THE MOON

THE HORRORS OF SOBOLTON BOOK SIX

AMY CROSS

This edition
first published by Blackwych Books Ltd
United Kingdom, 2024

Also available in e-book format.

www.amycross.com
www.blackwychbooks.com

CONTENTS

CHAPTER ONE
page 15

CHAPTER TWO
page 23

CHAPTER THREE
page 31

CHAPTER FOUR
page 39

CHAPTER FIVE
page 47

CHAPTER SIX
page 55

CHAPTER SEVEN
page 63

CHAPTER EIGHT
page 71

CHAPTER NINE
page 79

CHAPTER TEN
page 87

CHAPTER ELEVEN
page 95

CHAPTER TWELVE
page 103

CHAPTER THIRTEEN
page 111

CHAPTER FOURTEEN
page 119

CHAPTER FIFTEEN
page 127

CHAPTER SIXTEEN
page 135

CHAPTER SEVENTEEN
page 143

CHAPTER EIGHTEEN
page 151

CHAPTER NINETEEN
page 159

CHAPTER TWENTY
page 167

CHAPTER TWENTY-ONE
page 177

CHAPTER TWENTY-TWO
page 185

CHAPTER TWENTY-THREE
page 193

CHAPTER TWENTY-FOUR
page 201

CHAPTER TWENTY-FIVE
page 209

CHAPTER TWENTY-SIX
page 217

CHAPTER TWENTY-SEVEN
page 225

CHAPTER TWENTY-EIGHT
page 233

CHAPTER TWENTY-NINE
page 241

CHAPTER THIRTY
page 251

EPILOGUE
page 259

MAN
ON THE
MOON

CHAPTER ONE

Twenty years ago...

"WHAT ARE YOU DOING here?"

"Well, Lisa," Sheriff Joe Hicks replied, stepping forward and pushing past as he walked into her apartment and took a look around, "is there anything wrong with your friendly neighborhood law enforcement professional paying a house call? I'd have thought that in these trying and troubled times, that'd be seen as good service."

He turned to her.

"Are you experiencing trying and troubled times, Lisa?" he added pointedly.

Lisa opened her mouth to reply, before hesitating for a moment. She looked outside again, still keenly aware that she felt as if she was being watched, but there was no sign of anyone and she quickly realized that Joe's gaze was fixed on her very firmly. Her mind was racing and she still hadn't quite worked out what to do next about her memories of Michael and the wolves, but she knew for certain that Joe Hicks was the last person she could talk to about any of that; in fact, as she gently shut the door and turned to face him, she couldn't help but wonder whether he already knew about some of what had happened.

"Don't forget," Joe continued, with a faint smile as he studied her expression, "your father and I were very good friends, Lisa. Hell, I still remember the very last conversation I ever had with him, when he asked me quite specifically to keep an eye on you after he was gone."

"I don't need... keeping an eye on," she said cautiously.

"Oh, everyone does," he replied, turning and making his way across the room as if he was looking around for something. "Sometimes I think that's my job, really. People assume a sheriff's in place to maintain law and order, and that's certainly a part of it." He stopped and looked along the corridor that led to her bedroom. "But mainly, I think my job is to keep an eye on the town. Watch for trouble before it flares up."

He turned to her again.

"Are we on the same page?" he asked.

"Sheriff," she replied, trying to act naturally, "it's late and I'm pretty tired. I really think I just need to get some sleep."

"You know," he continued, "I've been keeping a particular eye on *you*, Lisa, and I just can't stop worrying. I think it's that report you turned in a while ago, the one about the wolves. I keep thinking that there must be more to it, that you of all people wouldn't turn in a report like that unless something else was going on." He took a couple of steps toward her again. "Now, I'm not doubting for one moment that you encountered a wolf, or some wolves, out there on the road leading out of town. What worries me is that this particular encounter might have dredged up some painful memories for you. Memories you'd rather leave in the past. Memories you *should* leave in the past."

"I'm really not sure that I know what you mean," she told him.

"And then there was that Wentworth Stone business," he added. "I started to see a narrative emerging. First the wolf thing, and then you seemed awfully destabilized when you were making all those wild accusations about Mr. Stone."

"I told you what I saw," she said firmly.

"And when I went to check it out," he replied, "there was nothing."

"Mr. Hicks, I don't know what you're getting at but -"

"Call me Joe," he added, cutting her off. "Come on, Lisa, where's all this Mr. Hicks stuff coming from? You know you can call me Joe."

"I just think -"

"Say it, Lisa," he continued. "Call me Joe."

She sighed.

"Call me Joe," he said yet again, and now he sounded much more serious. "Do it, Lisa, just so that I know we're in the same wheelhouse here. I want to hear you call me Joe, so I know that you trust me."

"Alright, Joe," she replied awkwardly, "you might be right. I think the best thing is if I just sleep on it. I've been a little frazzled lately, I've probably been working too hard, and I guess it's possible that I'm not quite on top of things." She paused, hoping that she might be starting to persuade him. "You wouldn't believe some of the cases I've been dealing with lately, it's as if every cat, dog, chicken and guinea pig in the Sobolton area has decided to require my attention. Plus I had to cancel a lot of procedures during the recent power-cut, so I've got to catch up on all of that, which means working every hour that God sends."

She waited.

Joe merely stared at her.

"So," she continued with a nervous smile, "if you think I've even got so much as a spare second to sit around thinking about the past, or about Lakehurst or any of that stuff, then you couldn't be more wrong. Right now, all I can think about is my workload for tomorrow, so I hope you won't take this the wrong way, but I really think that I just need to hit the hay." In an attempt to drive that point home, she headed to the door and pulled it open again, while desperately hoping that Joe would leave her alone. "Please, you mustn't think that I'm being rude. I'm sure you've got far more interesting things to deal with than my sorry work-life balance."

She turned to see that Joe was still standing in the middle of the room, showing no obvious suggestion that he might be about to leave. Although she wanted to keep talking, to find some way to *make* him leave, for a few seconds she really couldn't think of anything else to say.

"Well," Joe replied finally, putting his hands on his hips, "you've given me a lot to think about there, Lisa. A great deal. I just can't quite get past the feeling that everything's not quite on the up-and-up, if you catch my drift."

He wandered back toward the corridor that led down to the bedroom. He looked toward the doors at the far end, and then he turned to Lisa again.

"You know I've always had your back, don't you?" he continued. "Even twenty years ago, when your dear departed father was panicking about your troubles, I'm the one who pulled a few strings and made sure you got the treatment you so desperately required. I wasn't even sheriff back then, although I sure had my eye on the top job. Took me two more decades to get into position, but I managed that because I built a history of helping people out. But there's something more important than that, Lisa. From an early age, I've known about the dividing line between the forest and the town, and I've always had a keen eye on the need to balance those two conflicting interests. They can't mix, because do you know what happens when they *do* mix?"

Lisa tried to work out how best to answer that question. Before she had a chance, however, she realized that she could see a shadow moving in the corridor behind Joe, as if a figure was slowly stepping toward him.

"Chaos," Joe added. "I've seen it first-hand,

with my own eyes. That's why I'm the best person to... massage the situation so that everyone's happy. Now, establishing a balance doesn't mean making everything stay the same all the time. Sometimes it means a little quid pro quo. Do you know what that phrase means, Lisa? It's Latin, or something like that."

Swallowing hard, Lisa saw that the shadowy figures was still creeping up behind Joe, who seemed to have no idea that it was there at all.

"It means that sometimes the town takes something," Joe continued, slowly reaching for his gun, "and sometimes the forest takes something, and so long as the balance remains in the bigger picture, that's fine for -"

Suddenly he pulled his gun and turned, ready to fire. Before he had a chance, however, the figure grabbed him by the shoulders and threw him across the room, sending him smashing into the opposite wall.

Horrified, Lisa pulled back into the corner and watched as Joe tried to get to his feet; moving too fast to be seen properly, the figure raced over and hauled Joe up, knocking the gun from his hand before throwing him again, this time against one of the other walls. Letting out an angry cry, the figure immediately clambered over the furniture and threw itself down onto Joe, grabbing him by the throat and letting out a primal snarl before bringing its fists crashing down against Joe's face over and over, as if trying to beat the life out of him.

CHAPTER TWO

Today...

"WE'RE DEALING WITH AN animal," John said as soon as he entered the office, where all the other officers had gathered to receive their instructions. "We're dealing with someone who has no limits. No boundaries. No sense of right or wrong."

"Is there any news about Tommy?" Sheila asked, her voice tense with fear. "Did you speak to the hospital?"

"Tommy's still in critical condition," John said, stopping behind his desk and looking at the assembled group just as Robert Law finally caught up, entering the room while leaning heavily on his walking stick. "He's in the best hands at Middleford

Cross, though, so we have to focus on catching whoever did this to him."

"Do we have any leads?" Toby asked.

"The power-cut meant that no surveillance cameras were working at the time of the attack," John explained, "and it's going to take a while to check cellphone records from the area, although I'm not holding out much hope in that department. But whoever did this has to have left a trail. Someone must have seen them elsewhere in the town, and we're running on the hypothesis that this is the same person who attacked me a while back. I don't think this is someone local. I think it's someone from out of town."

"So which town *is* he from?" Sheila said. "Is there some kind of way we could try to liaise with -"

"My working hypothesis," John continued, interrupting him, "is that this is someone who's come out from the forest. I know that might sound strange, but we've received reports of someone possibly living out there, and I'm increasingly confident that there's some kind of connection."

"But the forest is huge," Wallace pointed out. "Boss, we can't search the entire forest. It's impossible."

"Plus we've always kind of avoided going

out there too much," Kelly stated.

John turned to her.

"Under Joe, I mean," she continued nervously, looking around at her fellow officers as if she was hoping for a little support. "I don't want to speak out of turn, it's just that Joe always used to tell us that our jurisdiction kind of ended where the forest begins. I know it doesn't literally end there, but he always said that anything from the forest was kind of... not our business."

"Joe ran things his way," John replied, bristling at everything he'd just heard, "and I run things *my* way." He paused for a moment. "Besides, I'm not sending anyone out there into the wilderness. You're right, that's an impossible task, it'd be like hunting for a needle in a haystack."

"Plus there are wolves in the haystack," Robert added.

"Exactly," John continued. "So here's what we're going to do. If this bastard came out of the forest, and went back in there, he has to have left a trace. I don't know what that trace might be, but that's where I'm relying on you guys. I want you to split into teams of two and check the entire perimeter of the town. Look for any sign of something moving between the town and the forest, and -"

Before he could finish, the lights briefly flickered as if they might be about to go out entirely. John looked up at the light above his desk, which continued to flicker for a few more seconds before stabilizing again.

"That'd be just what we need," Toby said. "Another power-cut."

"There's not going to be another power-cut," John said firmly. "Not tonight. Tonight we're going to be hunting this monster down, and I hope I don't need to remind you all that this is personal. One of our own is fighting for his life in the hospital, and it's our duty to catch whoever put him there. Before I came back to the station tonight, I talked to Tommy's wife and I promised her that we're going to get this son of a bitch. I made that promise on behalf of everyone in this room right now, and I don't know about the rest of you but I for one intend to keep that promise. And now, if there are no more questions, it's time for us to get to work."

***

"These maps mark the boundary between the town and the forest," John said, hurrying through to the reception area with a set of maps in his hand, then quickly setting the maps on a nearby table, "and -"

Stopping suddenly, he saw a sobbing Carolyn sitting behind the desk, dabbing at the front of her shirt.

"Are you okay?" he asked as the other officers caught up and began to take the maps.

"No!" Carolyn hissed angrily, slamming a set of paper towels down onto the desk. "Look at me! Why does that coffee machine in the break room hate me so much? Every single day now it spits coffee at me, no matter what I try to do! It's like it's gunning for me and trying to spray me with coffee whenever I try to use it and..."

She burst into more sobs, and although she was still trying to speak, her words were becoming increasingly unintelligible.

"Okay," Robert said, limping around behind the desk and putting a hand on her shoulder, "I think perhaps you need to take a little break."

"I can't," Carolyn whimpered. "Tommy's in the hospital and I just feel so powerless to do anything to help him!"

"Well, you can't do much if you're exhausted and covered in coffee," Robert told her. "Listen, why don't you let me drive you home? You can try to get some sleep, and then in the morning you'll be in a much better position to give it your all."

"I just hate that something like this could have happened to him," she replied, sniffing back more tears. "Tommy's the nicest man I've ever met in my life. He has a wife and a son, he has everything to live for, and now he might not even make it through the night."

"Let's just stay positive," Robert replied, before glancing at John. "Listen, I'm going to drive Carolyn home. I also know for a fact that I'll be no help out there in the search, I'd just slow everything down, so I'm not going to interfere. Instead I think I'll head back to the hospital and see if there's anything I can do there. Middleford Cross only reopened recently after being closed for a few years following an... incident a while back. Some of the guys there are still finding their feet, and I might be useful. Or not. Either way, I have to try."

"That sounds like a good plan to me," John said as the last of the officers headed out through the station's front door. "I need everyone to be where they're most useful."

"I just need to get my coat," Carolyn sobbed, standing up and heading through to the back room. "I hate that coffee machine! It's like it's out to get me!"

Once she was gone, John and Robert stood in silence for a moment.

"This isn't your fault, you know," Robert said finally. "I heard what you said at the hospital, and I just want you to understand that you have no responsibility for what happened to Tommy tonight."

He waited for an answer, but he could already see the sense of guilt in John's eyes.

"John -"

"I left him out there," John said, cutting him off. "I was supposed to have someone relieve him, but I was so busy with everything else that I forgot."

"So then someone else would have ended up in Tommy's place," Robert pointed out. "Who would you rather it had been? Toby? Sheila? Wallace? Corey? If you could change things so that someone else ended up meeting that monster, who would you choose?" He paused for a moment. "Believe me, John, I know what it's like to have to make difficult decisions. That's actually something I want to talk to you about, but I guess it can all wait until tomorrow."

"Is it related to what's happening tonight?"

"Not as far as I'm aware," Robert admitted, "but it might be relevant to the Lisa Sondnes case. Probably not, but in the interests of full disclosure, I should tell you that -"

"Sir?" Toby called out, hurrying to the doorway and stopping, clearly shocked by something. "We just got a call from someone who lives out toward the edge of town. They found... something."

"What?" John asked, ignoring Robert entirely as he headed over to the doorway. "Is it related to Tommy?"

"Yeah," Toby said, looking a little pale now, "and... Doctor Law, you might want to come out to take a look with us. It's kind of in your wheelhouse."

CHAPTER THREE

Twenty years ago...

"STOP!" LISA SCREAMED. "MICHAEL, don't kill him!"

Letting out an angry snarl, Michael gripped the sides of Joe's head and stared down at the unconscious man's face. He adjusted his hold, getting ready to squeeze tight and crack his victim's skull, but a moment later Lisa's hand touched his shoulder and he pulled back.

"Michael," she continued, her voice trembling now with shock, "I need you to listen to me. You can't kill him. Please, I'm begging you..."

"He was going to hurt you," he replied, as flakes of skin fell away from his bloodied face. "I could sense it in him. He was going to do something bad."

"That doesn't mean you have to kill him," she pointed out, keeping her hand on his shoulder in the hope that she might be able to calm him down. "He's in a pretty bad way already, Michael. Please, just... pull back."

Michael hesitated for a moment longer, still shaking with anger, before finally letting go of Joe's head. As the sheriff slumped down against the floor, Michael took a few steps back and tried to get himself under control; he glared at the man at his feet, clenching his fists, and then he turned to see the shocked expression on Lisa's face. He wanted to say something, to apologize for all the damage he'd caused in her apartment, but he was still coming to terms with the fact that – after so many years – they were face-to-face again.

"What happened to you?" she stammered, looking him up and down but quickly peering once more at his bloodied, damaged face and his hairless head. "Michael, you look..."

"Awful?" he asked, as flakes of dead skin fell from his cheek. "I can't say the same for you, Lisa. Somehow you're even more beautiful than you were when I first met you."

"I didn't remember you," she told him,

taking a step back. "Twenty years ago, my dad sent me away and I had treatment that messed with my head. By the time I came back, it was all gone. I knew something was wrong, that something was missing, but I had no idea that it was so important. It's been coming back slowly, especially recently. Eventually I found your cabin again, but -"

"I was there," he said, cutting her off. "I couldn't believe it when you walked back in. I so nearly spoke to you, but instead I hid." He paused. "I've been hiding a lot," he explained. "I've been watching over you, Lisa. For the past twenty years I've been watching you and keeping you safe, even when you were with that other guy I didn't take it personally, I knew that you had your reasons. I knew you'd forgotten me and I thought that might be for the best, but I still didn't want to leave you unprotected."

He looked around.

"I even came in here sometimes," he added. "Just to remind myself of your scent. I couldn't bear to forget that."

He touched the counter; when he pulled his hand away, a few flakes of dead skin remained on the surface.

"What happened to you?" Lisa asked again. "You look so different."

"The last time you saw me," he replied, "I'd just been attacked by my brother. I was badly hurt, and I had to shift to my wolf form so that the damage would be undone. That's a little trick that my species possesses. You have to believe me, Lisa, I had no choice, but I saw the horror in your eyes when you finally saw what I am. I saw the terror and the fear, and after I changed to my human form again and took you home, I swore that I'd never look that hideous again. So for the past twenty years, I've refused to go back to being a wolf. I won't do it ever again, not after the way you reacted."

He held his hands up, revealing the blistering sores that covered his entire body.

"Unfortunately," he added, "my body doesn't like that very much. My species is supposed to change periodically, so remaining in one form for so long... it's hard, but I don't mind the pain. I refuse to ever again become the thing that upset you so much."

He waited for a reply, but now she seemed to be lost for words.

"I shouldn't be here," he said suddenly, turning and heading toward the door. "It was a mistake coming here tonight, but I could sense that the sheriff was up to something bad. I just -"

"Don't go!" she replied, hurrying over and putting a hand on the side of his arm. "Michael, after everything that's happened, you can't possibly walk out like this. Where would you even go? Back into the forest?"

"It's where I belong," he replied, resisting the urge to turn to her. "Any time I come to the human world, I'm very much aware that I'm just an interloper. An invader. I don't belong here."

"I've only just remembered you," she pointed out, still touching his arm. "Michael, I have so many questions. My head's spinning right now and I'm not even sure that all my memories are back yet. Some of them are a little murky, so I think I need your help to pull them out better. Can you do that for me, Michael? I know I'm asking a lot, and I understand if you're mad at me for forgetting everything, but I really need your help to make sure that I remember everything that happened to me. Can you stay, at least for a while?"

"I never intended to let you see me again," he told her. "You have to believe me."

"I do," she said, "but this entire situation is crazy and I really need to know why all of this happened. I feel as if a huge part of my life has been ripped away, and I *need* to know the truth. Can you help me with that?"

She waited for an answer, but a moment later she heard a faint groaning sound coming from the other side of the room. Glancing over her shoulder, she saw that Joe Hicks was starting to stir; trying not to panic, she stepped away from Michael and headed across the room, and she looked down just in time to see that Joe's eyes were slowly opening. Reaching up, he touched the side of his head, immediately wincing as he felt one of the many spots where Michael had made contact.

"We need to get him out of here," she stammered, turning to Michael. "I don't know how, but -"

In that moment, she saw that the apartment's front door had been left wide open, and that there was no sign of Michael at all. She hesitated for a moment before hurrying over to the doorway and looking out across the parking lot, but already she could tell that he'd taken the opportunity to slip away.

"Michael!" she called out, hoping against hope that he might return. "Come back! You can't just leave like this!"

She waited, but a moment later she heard a long, slow groan emerging from Joe's lips. She turned to see that he was sitting up, and she felt a sliver of dread in her chest as she realized that she might have to start explaining herself. In their brief struggle, Michael and Joe – well, Michael really – had pretty much entirely trashed the apartment, and as Joe turned to her Lisa realized that she'd never be able to talk her way out of trouble. Not this time.

"Hey," she said cautiously, "what -"

"What happened?" he asked groggily, trying to get to his feet before slumping back down as if he was a little too dizzy. "Lisa, what am I... I don't quite remember..."

Realizing that she might have struck lucky, she made her way over and took his hand, helping him up and onto the sofa.

"I don't quite remember how I got here," he murmured, rubbing one side of his head again. "What in the name of all that's holy is going on here?"

"You disturbed an intruder," she told him.

"I did?" He looked up at her, as a trickle of blood ran down from a cut on his forehead. "Where is he now?"

"He... got away."

"He did, huh? I guess there's a first time for everything." He winced again. "I'm sorry, Lisa, I feel like I've let you down. Damn it, I can't believe the bastard gave me the slip. Excuse the language."

"Let me grab something so I can clean you

up," she replied, feeling relieved as she headed to the bathroom. "I'll be back in a moment."

"Take your time," he said, turning to watch as she disappeared along the corridor, then taking a moment to look around the overturned apartment as his eyes narrowed slightly. "An intruder, huh?" he whispered under his breath. "Well, Lisa, that's an odd way of phrasing it. Did you really think I wouldn't recognize your old boyfriend?"

CHAPTER FOUR

Today...

"ARE THOSE..."

John's voice trailed off for a moment as he watched Robert using a pair of tweezers to pick up the bloodied item from the ground.

"Is that a..."

"It's an eyeball, alright," Robert muttered, turning the object around as the optic nerve hung down. "Or what's left of it, at least. Looks like it's been crudely torn out from the socket."

"Is it... Tommy's?" Toby asked from a little further back.

"Unless you know anyone else who's going around losing eyeballs tonight," Robert replied, "I'd hazard that's a good guess. Quite why the assailant brought it all the way out here is no -"

Before he could finish, Toby turned and threw up on the muddy ground near the start of the treeline.

"My sentiment exactly," Robert said, rolling his eyes.

"We're right at the start of the forest," John pointed out, looking over at the dark space beyond the trees. "This is no coincidence. It's almost as if he put the eyeball here as a kind of marker."

"Come again?" Robert asked as Toby continued to throw up nearby.

"A little like the gate we found in the forest a while back," John continued, watching the forest. "They put a lot of importance on the idea of boundaries."

"They?"

"These people," John added, before stepping past Robert and picking his way across the grass at the side of the road. "Whatever you want to call them."

"What do *you* want to call them?" Robert asked.

Ignoring the question for a moment, John was already approaching a small bloodied item that he'd spotted near the base of one tree. Sure enough, as he got closer and crouched down to take a look, he saw a second partially burst eyeball in the dirt.

"I found the other one," he called over to

Robert. "He didn't just randomly rip them out from Tommy's face. It was part of a ritual."

"I'm not going to doubt you for one moment," Robert told him, "but what exactly would be the point of that particular ritual? I've got to admit, in all my time here I've never seen anything quite so gruesome." He paused for a moment. "Well, I've seen things that come close, but this is particularly nasty. I suppose people getting entirely ripped apart by wolves might be a tad higher on the scale."

"He would have put these here as he crossed from the human world to the forest," John mused, using a pen to pick up the second eyeball, "which at least tells us that this is the point at which he crossed over." He looked between the trees again. "So when he left the town," he continued, "he headed northwest, out not that far past Cutter's Hill. So we can assume that wherever he was going must be somewhere out in that direction, but what is there to the northwest that could possibly be his destination? As far as I'm aware, there's nothing out there but mile after mile of forest."

"And Drifter's Lake," Robert pointed out.

John turned to him, as Toby vomited again.

"It's sort of that way, at least," Robert continued.

"Is there anything else out there?" John asked. "Can you think of anything that might be relevant?"

"Maybe," Robert replied cautiously, leaning on his stick as he slowly got to his feet with the first eyeball still squeezed in the tweezers' tip. "It's a big forest. But John, my place is literally two minutes from here. If you're gonna do what I think you're gonna do, then I've got to insist that we pop by there first. There's something I want to give you."

***

"I feel a lot better now, thank you," Toby said as he sat in an armchair in the corner of the front room. "I don't think I'm going to..."

He hesitated, and then he muttered something unintelligible as he jumped to his feet and raced back to the bathroom. A moment later, he could be heard throwing up again.

"At least he made it," Robert said as he took a box down from the top of the bookshelf and set it on his dining room table. "My cleaner doesn't come until Monday. I'd have hated to have had to live with the stain until then."

"You have a cleaner?" John replied, making his way over to watch as Robert opened the box.

"You think I'm getting down on my knees to scrub the floor at my age?" Robert asked. "No way. I'd much rather pay Muriel to do that for me. Besides, she needs the money. Her Bess is having a baby soon and the father's run off, so they're scrimping and saving." He took out a smaller box from inside the larger one. "To be honest, Muriel doesn't even do the best job these days, she's definitely slacking, but I can't bring myself to fire her or to give her a nudge. And she does alright."

"Is this going to take long?" John asked. "I need to get back out there."

"I know you do," Robert replied, "and you're going to go alone, aren't you?"

"I -"

"Because you don't want another of your team to get hurt," he added, interrupting him. "I know you well enough by now, John, to figure out how your head's ticking. When you set them up to guard the perimeter of the town, that was partly to see if they found anything but also because you wanted to make sure that none of them went stumbling off into danger in the forest. Admit it."

"That thought... might have crossed my mind."

"And you still blame yourself for what happened to Tommy tonight," Robert continued, "even though I've explained to you why that's a foolish notion. But you won't listen to me, and I fully understand that, so I'm not gonna keep ringing the same bell. Instead, I'm going to give you the one thing that might actually help you out there."

"I'm not sure that I follow."

"These," Robert said, taking a small bag from the smaller box. "Hold out your hand."

"But -"

"Hold out your damn hand, John."

John did as he was told, and he watched as Robert tipped half a dozen silver bullets into his palm.

"I wish I had more for you," Robert continued, "but this'll have to do. Use them sparingly. They're not silver-tipped like your cheap rubbish, they're proper silver bullets that'll do serious damage. Just one of these should drop one of those things to the ground and keep him there."

"And why would I need silver bullets?" John asked.

"You know damn well why," Robert replied, meeting his gaze as they both heard Toby still throwing up in the bathroom. "You're going out there alone into the forest and I can't stop you. You're gonna head up toward Cutter's Hill and you're gonna keep going. There's almost a full moon tonight, so that'll help. But you're gonna go out there, and you've got good instincts so I won't be surprised if you find some way of tracking down whoever attacked Tommy tonight. I just want you to not be defenseless when that happens."

"But why *silver* bullets?" John said cautiously.

"You know why," Robert said firmly. "Do

you want to have a long, drawn-out conversation about it, or do you just wanna take the damn things?"

John opened his mouth to reply, before – thinking better of that idea – dropping the bullets into his pocket.

"Thank you," he said softly.

"I know you don't necessarily believe in all this stuff," Robert continued, "and I don't blame you for that approach. Not one bit. But at least keep an open mind, and consider the possibility." He paused again. "I started my career at a psychiatric hospital, John. It wasn't round here, but it was a strange old place with more than its fair share of ghosts and other oddities. I'm not gonna go into detail, but let me tell you that my eyes were opened by my time there and I saw things that I honestly can't explain. So that's how I know that there are things in this world that can't be understood by our petty little squishy brains. All we can do is accept that they're out there, and try to prepare ourselves accordingly. Do you get where I'm coming from with this?"

"I think so," John replied.

"If you go out to the woods tonight," Robert said, "and if you go alone, then at least be ready for anything. I've come to quite like you, John, and I think you're good for this town. I don't want you dying on us just yet."

"I'll try not to," John told him, before

checking his watch, "but if you don't mind, I think I need to get going."

"I'll drop Chucky off on my way to the hospital," Robert replied.

"Who?"

"Chucky." In the bathroom, Toby was still throwing up. "Chucking up? Get it?" Sighing, he shook his head. "My attempt at a little levity there, John," he admitted. "You can't blame me for trying to lighten the mood. Just promise me that you'll look after yourself tonight. We've already had one man get himself ripped apart by wolves recently. Having it happen again would be downright irresponsible."

CHAPTER FIVE

Twenty years ago...

"I'M FINE, I PROMISE," Joe said, wincing yet again as he opened the car door and prepared to climb out. "You've been too kind, Lisa. Far too kind. This is all in a night's work for me."

"Wait there," she replied, climbing out from the other side of her rental car and making her way round, then helping Joe as he slowly and very awkwardly rose to his feet. "You're still a little unsteady. Tomorrow you really need to see the doctor."

"Oh, I'll mend," Joe muttered, sounding a little out of breath as he took a moment to lean against the side of the vehicle. "I'm tougher than I look, Lisa. I might not have been sheriff for very long, but I've got plenty of experience. Sometimes people see a guy who's carrying a little extra weight, and they think he's out of shape, but there's plenty of muscle under these layers. By morning I'll be right as rain."

"I should get going," she said, checking her watch.

"Got somewhere to be?"

"I just... need to clean my apartment up. Do you want me to walk you to your door?"

"No, I'll be fine," he said, swinging the car door shut before taking a few limping steps to the sidewalk. "You know, as strange as this might sound, I still don't quite remember how I ended up at your place tonight." He stopped and turned to her. "I think I must have taken a real old bump on the old noggin, because for the life of me I don't remember anything between leaving the station and waking up on the floor of your apartment. Did you call me?"

She shook her head.

"Then what exactly happened?" he asked. "Did I just happen to swing by, and did you just happen to have some intruder at your place at the same time?"

"Coincidences happen," she told him, forcing a smile. "I'm just so relieved that you turned up at all, Joe. Honestly, I hate to think what might have happened if you hadn't."

"And do you really not have a description of the guy?"

"It was all a blur, really," she continued. "He was... big. And tough. Very strong. To be honest, I'm not sure I could have fended him off for much longer."

"Did I give as good as I got?"

"Absolutely."

"Sounds about right," he said, nodding knowingly. "I've still got a good left hook when I need it, Lisa. I used to box when I was younger and -"

"I really have to go," she replied, interrupting him as she hurried around to the other side of the car. "I'm sorry, Joe, but I'll call you real soon and answer any other questions you might have. I might not be around much tomorrow, but I'll be back in a day or two."

"Back?" he said, raising both eyebrows. "From where?"

Freezing for a moment, she stared back at him.

"Are you off on vacation?" he asked innocently, rubbing the side of his head again.

"Just a... business trip," she said cautiously. "I mean, the timing sucks, right? But I'll just have to tidy my apartment up when I get home. You know what they say. There's no rest for the wicked."

Joe took a step back and watched as she

clambered into the vehicle. The car's wheels spun slightly as Lisa floored the throttle, and Joe was left standing along as she drove away at full speed. Once she'd disappeared into the night, Joe rubbed the back of his head, clearly still in a little pain.

"Lisa Sondnes," he said under his breath, with a hint of bitterness starting to seep into his voice. "I never had you down as such a pathetic liar."

***

Slamming her foot on the brake pedal, Lisa brought the car screeching to a halt at the side of the pitch-black road. She switched the engine off, and then – as she looked out at the dark forest – she realized that more and more memories were flooding back.

"Who are you?" she remembered asking Michael when they'd first met.

"Are we doing names now?" he'd replied. "My name is Michael. And your name is..."

"Lisa," she'd told him, before deciding to lie. "Lisa... Smith."

"Hello, Lisa Smith," he'd continued. "You were in a pretty sorry way when I came across you in the forest. I'm afraid I left your bike out there. At least, I assume it belongs to you. It seemed to be in a pretty bad way and I needed to get us moving quite quickly. Carrying the bike as well as you would have slowed us down considerably."

"You carried me here?"

"I had to take a slight detour, as well," he'd admitted, "just to avoid certain... routes."

"How did I forget?" she whispered now, as a shudder passed through her bones. "How could I possibly have forgotten something so important?"

"We don't always get what we want, Lisa," she remembered Doctor Campbell telling her, back in his office at Lakehurst. "You have to understand that from the moment you walked through the front door here, you entered a treatment plan that has to be pursued to its natural conclusion. There's no hopping off midway through."

"I didn't *walk* through the door," she'd insisted angrily. "I was dragged, kicking and screaming against my will. What law gives you the right to hold me here against my will?"

"You've responded well to your treatment so far," he'd explained confidently, with the tone of someone who felt as if he was completely in control, "but I think a higher dosage might be worth trying. We're still well within the margin for error, and you've shown very few negative side-effects so far. In fact, your resilience is remarkable."

And then there had been the treatment, so many rounds of electric shock therapy that had zapped her brain until every trace of Michael had been gone. Or, if not gone, then at the very least deeply suppressed until she had no idea it was even missing; it had all been there, though, bubbling away beneath the surface and waiting for some cue that might bring it back. That cue, she realized now, had been her encounter with the wolf cubs on an icy road beyond the edge of town, and then the moment when she'd spotted the man who'd been trying to take the cubs away. She remembered the way his body had twisted and contorted, and she understood now that he must have been like Michael; he'd been changing, turning into a wolf, and from that moment she'd been on the path back to uncovering the truth about her past.

"I'm only trying to help you," she imagined her father saying.

Looking at the mirror, she saw his face reflected from the back seat. She knew he wasn't really there, that he was just a ghost now, one she carried everywhere she went, but she still bristled at the sight of him.

"If you were real," she said through gritted teeth, "I'd tell you right now that I'd never forgive you."

"Is that true?" he asked. "You were always my precious little girl, Lisa. You have to realize that I only ever -"

"You weren't trying to protect me!" she hissed.

"I -"

"You stole half my life!" she snarled. "You and Joe teamed up, and you sent me to that place so that you could have the truth ripped from my mind."

"You were in a terrible state," he told her. "Your life would have been ruined."

"You made me forget him," she said, with tears in her eyes.

"It was for the best."

"I loved him!" she shouted angrily, turning but seeing only the empty seat. She looked in the mirror again, but now the vision of her father was gone. "I loved him," she said again, as a shudder passed through her chest. "I really loved him."

Feeling as if she might be about to scream and never stop, she almost tripped as she climbed out of the car. She hurried around to the rear and opened the trunk, and she quickly pulled out her rifle and checked for any ammunition; she didn't have much, and after a moment she discovered that she had only one silver bullet. She held that bullet up for a moment, fully aware that it wouldn't be remotely enough if she happened to run into trouble, but at the same time she couldn't hold back. She was already making a mental map of the route back to the cabin, and she told herself that she had to find Michael. Besides, if she ran into difficulties, he'd protect her.

He'd *always* protected her.

AMY CROSS

CHAPTER SIX

Today...

"OKAY, I'M GOING TO drop you off here," Robert said, bringing his car to a halt at the side of the road, "and then I really need to get to the hospital. I know I won't be much use, but it's not as if I'll get any sleep at home. I might as well try."

"Thank you," Toby said, still sounding a little queasy as he sat in the passenger seat. "I feel so stupid, Doctor Law. I'm supposed to be out there with the others, helping to track down the monster that did all of this, and instead I'm letting the side down."

"Well, you need to think of it like this," Robert replied. "Everyone else – and I mean everyone – is out there right now conducting the search. So by the time morning comes, everyone's going to be exhausted. Except you. So you're going to collect your car from the lot over there, and you're going to drive home. You're going to get some sleep, and then in the morning you'll be fighting fit and ready to take over from the others. Doesn't that sound like a good idea?"

"I guess so," Toby said, although he didn't sound too certain.

"It's the best idea ever," Robert said, leaning over him and opening the door on the passenger side. "I see your car right there. It's the blue one, isn't it?"

Toby nodded.

"Go home," Robert continued, "and -"

Suddenly they both heard a loud banging sound coming from somewhere nearby. They turned and looked toward the pitch-black sheriff's station, and then – hearing the sound again – they both looked at the medical office at the side of the place.

"What was that?" Toby asked cautiously.

"I have no idea," Robert replied, "but... I think it's coming from *my* part of the building."

***

The door creaked open, revealing Robert and Toby standing on the step that led into the medical unit. They both looked along the corridor for a moment, before Robert leaned over and flicked a switch on the wall, bringing the strip lights flickering to life above.

"It sounds quiet now," Toby pointed out uncertainly. "Maybe it was just... the wind."

"Maybe."

"Or the building was settling."

Robert turned to him.

"Isn't that what happens in horror films?" Toby suggested. "Buildings settle and make weird noises. I've seen enough films to know that -"

"You're probably quite right," Robert replied, interrupting him. "Toby, listen, you've been through more than enough this evening already, so I really think you need to get home. Doctor's orders, and all that."

"But -"

"I'm just going to check on a few things here," Robert continued, patting him on the shoulder, "but I'll be fine. I need you to go to your car and drive yourself home immediately. You feel up to driving, don't you?"

"I... yes, but -"

"Then off you go," Robert said firmly. "You're not going to make me mention any of this to Sheriff Tench, are you?"

"I'm going," Toby muttered, turning and hurrying away. "I'm sorry, Doctor Law, I didn't mean to question your judgment. I'll get some rest and I'll be back first thing in the morning."

"Are you sure I'm not letting the side down?" Toby asked. "Because if I am, I can push through and keep going. I'm not afraid of hard work, and I'm sure I'll be okay just so long as I don't have to see more eyeballs. I don't know what it was about them, but they just made me want to -"

Stopping suddenly, he seemed to be on the verge of throwing up again.

"Don't even think about any of that," Robert said firmly, keen to get rid of him. "Do I have to write a proper note on headed paper, ordering you to go home? You're done here for tonight, Toby. Get some rest and come back when you're useful in the morning."

"Okay," Toby said, still clearly a little uncertain. "Whatever you think's best, Doctor Law."

"You do that," Robert replied, watching as he disappeared around the corner, then looking along the corridor again. "You get yourself off somewhere safe, Toby. Like any sensible person."

He waited, and after a moment he heard a brief bumping sound coming from somewhere else in the building. Swallowing hard, he tried to convince himself that he was just imagining things, but deep down he knew that he couldn't simply turn and walk away. As much as he wanted to get to Middleford Cross and try to help the team that was working on Tommy, after a few seconds he leaned on his walking stick as he stepped into the corridor and pulled the door shut.

After listening for a few seconds, he began to make his way toward the double doors at the far end. His knee was hurting again, and he hated the fact that he was so slow and immobile, but he also knew that he had a duty to check that nothing was wrong. Whoever had attacked Tommy was far away by now, of that he was certain, but deep down – even if he didn't want to admit the fact – he knew full well what had caused the initial banging sound that he and Toby had heard from the car outside.

He just wanted to prove to himself that he was wrong.

Reaching the double doors, he hesitated for a moment longer before gently pushing them open. He looked through into the next corridor and saw that so far everything seemed to be completely in order, but a few seconds later he heard a sudden thud coming from one of the rooms to the right. He turned and looked at the nearest door, and already he could feel a churning sense of dread in the pit of his belly. Part of him knew full well that he was being a fool, that he should get out of the place and call for back-up, but he also knew that everyone from the station – apart from Toby, at least – was at that moment engaged in the search around the town's perimeter. Sure, he could try to persuade one of them to help, but he also didn't want to come across as a complete fool.

He stepped over to one of the doors and reached for the handle, and then he forced himself to push the door open and switch the next light on. He was in the waiting room next to the examination area now, and so far every fresh noise served only to confirm his early suspicions. Looking over at the glass-paneled door that led through to the storage area, he could feel his heart pounding but he knew that he had to keep going. He began to cross the room, pushing through the pain in his knee and hip, and finally he opened the next door and switched on the next light.

And then he froze as he saw that his worst fear had come true: one of the cabinets in the far wall had been forced open, with the door slightly twisted as if it had been smashed from the inside.

Stepping forward, John already knew which cabinet had been damaged, but he had to be certain. Making his way closer, he saw that the metal tray had been partially extended, and when he checked the tag on the front of the broken door he saw the three letters that he'd known were going to be there all along.

L.M.D.

Little Miss Dead.

Or, as he'd scribbled beneath those letters a day or two earlier, Eloise.

Peering into the cabinet, he saw that the

dead girl was indeed missing. He looked at the inside of the metal door and saw a series of heavy dents, and he couldn't ignore the fact that these dents appeared to have been made from the inside; the latch had been smashed away and left partly dangling from the door, but again this made no real sense since the cabinets themselves weren't kept locked and anyone could have simply pulled one of them open from the inside.

Unless they were trying to force their way *out.*

A moment later he heard a creaking sound coming from the next room. He looked over at the open door, and he realized that he remembered closing that door when he'd left earlier. He limped across the room as he heard the creaking sound again, and then he switched on another light and found himself looking into the the little preparation room at the very rear of the building. The back door, which led out to the side of the parking lot, was wide open, and he watched with a growing sense of horror as the door swung gently in the wind, causing the hinges to let out a familiar creaking sound.

Down on the metal floor, meanwhile, faint traces of a child's footprints could be seen leading from the spot where Robert was standing to the open door and out toward the parking lot.

AMY CROSS

CHAPTER SEVEN

Twenty years ago...

"I'M COMING!"

As soon as he managed to unlock the front door to the station, Joe realized he could hear the phone ringing in his office. He'd noticed the sound from outside, but now he was certain that it was coming from one room in particular. He flicked the lights on in the reception area before shuffling along the corridor, walking as fast as he could manage while wincing as he felt stiff pains in his legs. He hadn't wanted to show any weakness to Lisa, but he had to admit that the encounter in her apartment had left him feeling pretty rough.

"Hold your horses," he snapped as he limped into his office.

He hesitated for a moment, staring at the phone on his desk, and then he grabbed the receiver and held it up to his ear.

"What do you want?" he asked. "If it's about the girl, I already -"

"I didn't think I'd ever have to make this call," the voice on the other end of the line replied, cutting him off. "I thought you'd be able to keep things under control."

"It's just a small hiccup," Joe replied. "You just need to give me some time to get everything sorted out."

"Time's one thing we don't really have," the voice replied. "Do you realize how serious this matter has become? I was willing to give you the benefit of the doubt earlier, Sheriff Hicks, but you seem to be losing your grip on the situation. I'm starting to wonder whether I was right to support your bid for the top job."

"Of course you were right," he stammered, struggling to hide a sense of irritation. "What exactly are you implying? That I'm some kind of idiot?"

"The girl is heading out to the forest now," the voice sneered. "She remembers."

"I couldn't help that," Joe spat.

"But you saw it coming, didn't you?"

"I hoped I was wrong," Joe continued, before allowing himself a heavy sigh. "I hoped that what we did twenty years ago might have been enough."

"I have enough trouble," the voice replied, "maintaining order between my sons. They don't make things easy for me, but I was hoping that you'd at least keep the girl away. The situation was tenable but now I fear that it's all starting to unravel. If she returns to see him, then -"

"I'll fix it!" Joe snapped angrily.

"How?"

"I'll..."

For a moment Joe's voice trailed off, as he realized that his initial idea – to send Lisa back to Lakehurst – probably wasn't going to be enough. He knew what the voice really wanted, but his friendship with Rod Sondnes was causing him to try to come up with some other plan. Finally, however, he reminded himself that the town of Sobolton was far more important than the life of any one person.

"I'll take care of it tonight," he whispered.

"The tone of your voice has changed. Does that mean -"

"It means I'll take care of it before the sun comes up," he said firmly. "You won't have to call again, not about this. And you won't have to get into my head, either. I promised you that I'd be the firm pair of hands you need, and that's not about to change. Don't look at this as a failure. Look at it as a chance for me to prove what I can do. By the time morning comes, everything will be settled again. I'll massage over the bumps."

"My time in this world is coming to an end," the voice replied. "I must be sure that my sons are fully grown by the time I depart. You understand my concern, do you not?"

"More than you can possibly imagine," Joe said darkly. "Don't worry about any of this. I'm on the case." He waited for an answer. "Do you understand? Are you still there? Hey, can you hear me or -"

Suddenly he let out a gasp as the receiver began to burn. He let go, and he watched as the receiver began to melt even as it landed on the desk. A moment later the phone itself began to spit and spark, finally bursting into flames. Shocked, Joe grabbed the fire extinguisher from the wall and pulled the pin, before spraying the desk and putting the fire out. Once he was done, he set the extinguisher aside and stepped back, leaning against the wall for a moment as he loosened the button on his collar.

"Okay, then," he said finally, sounding more than a little breathless. "We seem to have an understanding."

***

"Who's there?" Lisa gasped, raising the rifle as she

turned and looked back the way she'd just come. She aimed her flashlight between the darkened trees, but she saw no sign of anyone. "I'm armed," she continued. "If there's anyone here, don't think I won't use this thing."

She waited, but she heard only the sound of wind blowing through the forest, causing the treetops to sway high above. A moment earlier she'd heard the sound of a twig snapping, although now she found herself wondering whether she might have been mistaken. She swallowed hard, still watching the gaps between the trees, before slowly lowering the rifle again.

"Keep your head," she muttered under her breath, trying to stop herself panicking. "Whatever you do, just don't... start imagining things."

She paused for a moment longer, and now she was wondering whether Michael might have already sensed her presence in the forest. After all, now that she remembered him, she couldn't be sure about the limit of his abilities.

"Michael, are you there?" she asked. "If you are, can you just come out and talk to me? I really think we should be beyond the point of sneaking about. If you're upset that I forgot about you, I can only apologize again. It really wasn't my fault, it was just something that was done to me. I'm not even -"

Before she could finish, she heard another

splitting sound. She turned and aimed the rifle in the other direction, and now she felt absolutely certain that she had company. She adjusted her grip, but already she could tell that her hands were clammy, and she could feel her heart racing in her chest.

"Who's there?" she called out again, trying in vain to sound calm and collected. "Michael, is that you? Michael, if it's you, please just come out and talk to me. I really want to clear all of this up and try to figure out what's going on here. Now that I remember you..."

As her voice trailed off, she began to remember the excitement she'd felt twenty years earlier when she'd been so close to Michael. Although she hated to be disloyal, she knew now that Michael had made her feel a way that Wade had never managed, and that in some ways she'd already sensed with Wade that something was missing. Sure, she'd tried so hard to fall head over heels in love with Wade, yet now she understood that her feelings for Michael had always been holding her back. Somehow Michael had always been lurking in her heart, always waiting to emerge again.

Spotting something moving in the darkness ahead, she took a cautious step forward. Unable to resist the hope that Michael might be about to appear, she could already tell that the figure on the ground was no wolf; after another step, however, she realized that it also didn't appear to be entirely human. A moment later, as the flashlight's beam caught the creature's hunched back, she saw it turning to look at her, and she realized that she'd encountered this thing once before, on an icy road beyond the edge of town.

Slowly the creature turned fully toward her and let out a rumbling snarl. As it tried to stand, Lisa saw that this was the same figure she'd shot while it was in the process of changing its form. Part man and part wolf, like some kind of twisted amalgamation of the two, the figure took a stumbling step forward and snarled again, and Lisa saw a silver bullet still lodged deep in its flesh.

"Hey," she stammered, hoping against hope that she might be able to calm the situation down. She took a step back, while still holding the rifle up and wishing that she'd been able to find some more silver bullets. "Long time no see. I hope you're not too mad about what happened last time."

The creature took another step toward her, although it seemed to be having trouble staying upright.

"I can take a look at that, if you want," she continued, although she wasn't even sure that the creature could hear her. "I'm a veterinarian, and I could pull it out... I don't know if that'd help, but -"

Suddenly the creature lunged at her, slamming into her chest and sending her falling back against the ground. She tried to fire, but she only managed to shoot helplessly into the sky before the creature threw the gun out of her hands and reached its jaws down toward her bare throat.

CHAPTER EIGHT

Today...

"UH, HELLO?" ROBERT SAID, stepping out from the back of the building and looking across the station's parking lot. "Uh... little girl? Little Miss Dead?"

He paused, before remembering that she had a proper name now.

"Eloise?" he added hopefully, looking around in the darkness but seeing no sign of her. "Can you hear me? If -"

Stopping himself just in time, he quickly reminded himself that the girl was dead. Not only had she been found encased in the lake's ice, but there was also the small matter of the autopsy that he'd conducted; he'd removed all her organs, he'd taken her brain from her skull and weighed it, he'd made all sorts of cuts and incisions, and then he'd kept her refrigerated in one of the cabinets. There could simply be no way for her to still be alive, and he began to wonder instead whether she might have been stolen.

He turned to look at the other way, but the entire parking lot was empty and he couldn't even begin to imagine how anyone could have escaped with the dead girl in just a matter of minutes. That left the possibility that the thief might still be hiding inside the building somehow, so he turned to go back inside, only to freeze in his steps as he finally spotted a figure in the distance, standing at the very far end of the parking lot and seemingly staring up at the vast forest-covered hills that spread out beyond the edge of town.

The figure was short, and its plastic gown was flapping gently in the wind.

"Impossible," Robert whispered, as he felt a thud of shock punching him in the gut. "This can't be happening."

Leaning on his stick, he began to make his way across the lot, heading toward the figure. With each step he was able to see her a little better, and he could tell that she appeared to be the same little girl from the mortuary. He kept telling himself that he had to be wrong, that either he was suffering from some kind of psychotic episode or some bastard was playing a prank on him, but finally he stopped a few feet back from the girl and saw that there really could be no mistake.

"Impossible," he said again, his voice trembling now with fear. "I cut you open. I carried out an autopsy on you. I cracked open your ribs!"

Slowly she turned to face him.

"I took out your heart and your brain," he said through gritted teeth, "and I weighed them before I put them back inside you!"

His mouth hung open for a moment as the girl's dead eyes stared back at him. Her plastic gown was still blowing in the wind, but as he watched the girl Robert realized that something about her was different. She was so young, certainly pre-teen, but he'd never seen her features like this before. At first she'd been in the ice, then later her face had lost all muscle contraction on the mortuary table; only now was he seeing her face properly, as if would like when she was alive, and the change in her appearance was subtle but significant.

In that moment, as the girl turned to face him fully, Robert realized with a growing sense of horror that he recognized her all too well.

"It can't be you," he whispered, taking a step back. "It can't..."

His voice trailed off, but deep down he knew that he was right, and finally one name fell from his lips.

"Lisa?"

***

"It's not you!"

Slamming the door shut, Robert pressed himself against the frosted glass. He reached down and, with a fumbling hand, he managed to push the latch across so that the door to the mortuary was locked, and then he turned and took a few steps back along the corridor.

"It's not you," he continued, even as the girl's face continued to haunt his mind's eye. "That's not possible. Lisa Sondnes would be well into her fifties by now, and that's assuming she was still alive, which she clearly isn't but..."

He watched the window as a small figure began to approach from the other side. A moment later someone out there tried the handle; the door remained locked, but already Robert was thinking of all the other ways that someone might get into the building. There were a couple more doors in the mortuary itself, plus the entire wing was connected to the sheriff's station and he had no idea how many other doors might be waiting, and whether they were all sealed properly. Ordinarily there'd be someone else in the building, at least on the front desk overnight, but he knew for a fact that every available person was at that moment assisting in the hunt for Tommy's attacker.

Which meant -

Suddenly the lights went off, plunging the corridor into darkness.

"Another blackout?" Robert stammered, before hurrying through to his office and looking out at the parking lot.

To his relief, he saw that the lights were on in the rest of the town, but that relief quickly faded as he realized that this meant: someone had somehow managed to cut all the power to the sheriff's station.

"This isn't really happening," he said under his breath, hoping frantically that he might be about to wake up and discover that the entire situation was simply a nightmare. That, at least, would make a little sense.

He reached up and tested the window, making sure that it was securely locked. Slipping his phone from his pocket, he brought up John's number and tapped to call, and then he waited for the connection. After a few seconds, however, the call timed out; he tried again, with the same result, and he sighed as he realized that most likely John was out in the forest and beyond the reach of cellphone signals.

"Damn it," he muttered, bringing up Tommy's number, only to remember at the last moment that Tommy was definitely not going to be able to help.

He hesitated, before bringing up Carolyn's number so that he could at least ask her who the hell he needed to call. And then, as soon as he tapped to try this particular number, the phone exploded in a shower of sparks that sent him reeling back against the wall.

Letting out a gasp of pain, he looked down and saw that melted plastic was dripping from his hand, burning the skin. He wiped it away, but already the heat had caused a lot of damage, almost melting the flesh from his fingers. Blood was running down to his wrist, and a moment later he looked at the window again and saw the dead little girl staring in at him from outside.

"Leave me alone!" he yelled. "I haven't done anything wrong!"

He waited, clutching his injured hand, but the girl merely continued to watch him until finally he limped over and closed the blinds. At least now, even if she was still out there, he wouldn't be able to see the accusing glare in her eyes.

"It can't be you," he whispered, thinking back to the sight of the girl's face in the parking lot. "I would have noticed before. *Someone* would have noticed. It can't be you, because you vanished twenty years ago and you'd be too old now, and besides... your name isn't even Lisa, it's Eloise so -"

Suddenly he heard a thudding sound coming

from somewhere else in the building. He looked over his shoulder, and then – pulling the blinds open – he was shocked to find that the girl had vanished. A fraction of a second later he heard glass breaking in one of the other rooms, and after limping to the open door he looked along the corridor and realized that someone else was in the building now. He watched the empty corridor for a moment, until finally one of the doors began to creak open. A couple of seconds later, to his horror Robert saw the dead little girl stepping into view. Her plastic gown was torn now, clearly on the glass of a window, and she immediately turned and stared straight at Robert before he backed into his office.

"I don't believe it," he stammered, before pushing the door shut. Realizing that there was no way to lock it from the inside, he grabbed the bookshelf and began to drag it into place so that it would block the entrance further. "There's an explanation for all of this, I just have to keep my head straight until I figure out what it might be."

Hearing a bumping sound on the other side of the door, he pulled back just as the handle began to turn. Worried that the girl – who'd already forced her way out of a metal cabinet – might be able to break into the room, he pushed back against the bookshelf in a desperate attempt to make it stay in place.

"I know it's not you!" he shouted as the girl

pushed against the door's other side. "You can't be here! You're not real!"

CHAPTER NINE

Twenty years ago...

HEARING A SNARLING, SNEERING sound ringing out through the night air, Lisa immediately began to drag herself away from the creature. She let out a pained cry as she felt its claws scratching at her leg, but she finally managed to pull back just in time to see that two wolves were already fighting the creature off and forcing it back.

One of the wolves turned and growled, and in that moment Lisa saw that this was the same one-eyed wolf she'd first encountered so many years earlier. She knew there was no way the beast could still be alive after twenty years, but she quickly told herself that this wasn't the time to start debating the realities of the situation.

Instead she grabbed her rifle and stumbled to her feet. Making her way between two nearby trees, she turned and saw that the two wolves were already managing to drive the other creature away, almost as if they were shepherding it out of the picture. Raising her rifle, Lisa briefly considered taking a couple of shots at the animals, before realizing that her best bet might simply be to run while they were all busy fighting one another. As she turned and scrambled between the trees, she heard periodic yelps and cries of pain coming from somewhere over her shoulder, but she forced herself to keep going until finally all sounds of the fight seemed to be way off in the distance.

Exhausted, she stopped for a moment and leaned against a tree. She'd still just about managed to retain her bearings, and after a moment she realized that she knew which way to go if she wanted to reach the cabin. For the first time, however, she began to wonder whether she might be making a terrible mistake. Her life in Sobolton had felt so safe and secure, and now she found herself asking whether she should just go back to all of that and try to pretend that the mess in the forest had never happened at all. She still loved Michael, at least in some way, but she couldn't shake the sense that perhaps he wasn't good for her.

Had her father been right, all those years ago?

For a couple of minutes she remained firmly in place, unable to make her mind up. She was starting to shiver now in the cold night air, and she wondered whether she could ever leave Michael alone. If she went home and locked the door, and got on with her job, would the world of the forest simply leave her alone? It had certainly left her alone for two decades now, at least until she'd blundered her way back into the midst of it all; now that she knew the danger, she felt tempted to simply turn away and pretend that none of it existed.

Just like the rest of the town's population.

Finally, telling herself that she at least needed time to think, she turned to make her way back to the car. After just a couple of steps, however, she was startled by the sight of the one-eyed wolf standing directly ahead. With blood caked around its face, the wolf bared its teeth, snarling at her as if to warn her to stay back.

"I'm going!" she stammered, holding the rifle up for a moment, aiming at the wolf but trying to resist the urge to pull the trigger. "I don't want any trouble. I'm just leaving, that's all."

She waited, but to her surprise the wolf didn't attack this time; instead the creature simply continued to snarl, and a moment later the second wolf stepped into view a few feet to the right.

"Where's your other friend?" Lisa asked, looking around for some sign of the half-man, half-wolf creature she'd seen a few minutes earlier. "Did you chase him off?"

Again she waited, although she knew she was unlikely to get much of an answer. A moment later she tried to start making her way around the wolves, giving them a wide berth, but they both quickly moved so that they were once again in her way.

"Why aren't you attacking me?" she asked, but a moment later the answer emerged from the depths of her thoughts. "Do you want me to go the other way?" she continued. "Is that it? Do you *want* me to go toward the cabin?"

The one-eyed wolf let out a deeper, angrier snarl that served only to confirm Lisa's question.

"Okay, then," she said cautiously, unable to quite figure out what was happening, but starting to slowly back away between the trees while keeping the rifle raised. "Looks like you've got your way, at least for now. Just don't start anything with me!"

***

A short while later, still making her way through the forest, Lisa stopped and turned to look over her shoulder. For a moment she heard nothing in the darkness, but after a few more seconds the familiar sound returned once more: something was following her, making sure that she was on the right path.

She swallowed hard.

Every time she'd met the wolves before – particularly the beast with only one eye – they'd tried to attack her. This time they were acting very differently, acting almost as a guard of honor as if they were determined to lead her safely through the forest. Part of her worried that they were merely waiting for a better moment to strike, so that they could rip her apart without fear of being disturbed, but deep down she knew that wasn't quite the case; the two wolves, having saved her from the half-man half-wolf creature – genuinely seemed to be guiding her to some point. And as she looked around, she realized that she was getting closer and closer to Michael's cabin.

And that, she knew, couldn't be a coincidence.

"Still there, huh?" she said nervously, trying – and failing – to make light of the situation. She heard a scratching sound, an answer of sorts, and then she set off again.

After all, she knew she had no other choice now.

Eventually she reached the edge of the clearing and saw the cabin ahead. She felt her heart skip a beat; a single candle was burning in the window, and the place looked much more homely than it had during her recent visits. She'd been exploring the cabin for a while now, searching its darkest corners for scraps of memory, but now she remembered the good times she'd spent in the place with Michael twenty years earlier. She was tempted to think of the cabin as a kind of home away from home, but a moment later she spotted the shadow of a figure moving past one of the windows and she understood that a lot had changed over the course of two decades.

Hearing a faint growling sound, she turned and saw that the two wolves were a little closer now, evidently keen for her to keep going.

"Now you *want* me here?" she said, still trying to understand the pretty major change in their attitude. "A little consistency might be nice."

She knew that she had no other option, however, so after a moment she began to walk across the clearing, allowing the wolves to steer her toward the cabin's door. Her chest felt desperately tight with anticipation now, and that sensation only increased tenfold when – just a few seconds later – the cabin's front door opened to reveal Michael standing silhouetted against the flickering glow inside.

"Hey," she said, forcing a smile that felt distinctly unnatural.

She waited, but he said nothing; she wasn't entirely certain what she'd been expecting, but already she could sense an awkward atmosphere, and a moment later she heard a shuffling sound over her shoulder. She turned to see that the two wolves had emerged from the clearing, stepping into the moonlight and watching her as if they wanted to make sure she actually entered the cabin. Staring back at the wolf she'd come to nickname One-Eye, she felt certain that she could see the hatred in his features.

"I was given some company on the way here," she continued, turning to Michael again, then starting to make her way over to the cabin. "I don't know what changed, but it's almost as if they wanted me to get here. They actually saved me from something out there. That's another thing I need to ask you about, actually."

Stopping at the foot of the steps, she looked up and saw Michael's gaunt features. Even in the few hours since she'd last seen him, he seemed noticeably more troubled.

"You need to come inside," he said finally.

"What if -"

"You need to come inside, Lisa," he continued, stepping out of the way and gesturing for her to enter the cabin. "They won't tolerate you staying out there for much longer. I'm sorry, I wish there'd been some way to warn you but... I just couldn't. Not this time."

"What are you talking about?" she asked, making her way up the steps and then walking into the cabin. "What -"

Before she could finish, she heard the door swing shut behind her. She turned and saw that Michael was already looking out through one of the windows, watching the clearing as if he was scared. Heading over to join him, she looked out and saw that the two wolves were still in the clearing, almost as if they were standing guard.

"It's gone too far now," Michael said through gritted teeth. "I've been such a fool. Now he's going to come, and I don't know if I can stand in his way."

"Who?" Lisa asked. "Who's going to come?"

"Who else?" he asked darkly, before slowly turning to her with fear in his eyes. "My father."

CHAPTER TEN

Today...

"ANY LUCK?"

"Nothing," Garrett said, listening to the phone's voicemail message for a moment longer before sighing and cutting the call. "I don't get it. Doctor Law specifically told me to call him if we needed him. Now his phone seems to be off."

"Or out of signal," Jessie replied, stepping over and setting her clipboard down on the desk at the nurses' station. "Just give it a while and I'm sure he'll call back. Besides, it's not like it's an emergency. The patient's fairly stable now and before he left, Doctor Marshall said that we just need to -"

"I know what Marshall said," Garrett

snapped angrily, before taking a moment to compose himself. Looking past Jessie, however, he felt a sense of dread as he spotted the open door leading into room thirteen a little further along the corridor. "I just don't like it, that's all," he added. "Call it a gut thing, but I can't shake the feeling that something's really wrong."

"Welcome to the Overflow," she said with a grin, heading past him and stopping to check some details on the computer. "Or the Double Overflow, as some of us call it. The original Overflow was bad enough, but then some idiot decided to use public money to build a replacement." At that moment the lights briefly flickered. "Talk about a complete waste. There were so many crazy stories about the old hospital, and sometimes I feel like most of those stories have directly transferred over to the new place."

"Stories?" He turned to her. "What kind of stories?"

He waited, but he could tell that she seemed a little hesitant. After a moment, however, she stepped closer and glanced around as if she was worried that they might be overheard.

"I don't know the exact details," she whispered, "but somebody told me that about ten years ago some really crazy stuff happened at the old Middleford Cross. There was a fire at some point, and something about a nurse named Elly

Blackstock, and an oxygen tank..." Her voice trailed off for a moment. She looked around again. "Some of the stories get really insane if you listen to them, but most people prefer to keep their mouth shut. That's what makes me think there's some truth to it. I mean, if people keep yapping about something, you know it's probably a load of crap. But if they seem genuinely scared..."

"And do *you* believe this stuff?" he asked.

"Honey, I don't know what I believe," she replied, allowing herself a faint smile as she took a step back. "Can you go and check on that cop in room thirteen? Eventually that Doctor Law asshole's gonna show up and probably tear us all a new one, so we might as well at least have the paperwork in order. I know he said he was only going to be advising us, but I bet he'll cause trouble." She headed away along the corridor, before stopping as they both heard a loud bump coming from somewhere far off on the ward. Turning to Garrett, she smiled again. "You don't mind being left alone for a little while, do you?"

"Mind?" he said through gritted teeth. "Why would I mind."

"No reason," she continued, turning and walking away again. "You don't seem a like a jumpy guy, Garrett. Just watch out for the ghost of Priscilla Parsons!"

"The ghost of who?" he called after her,

watching as she made her way through the double doors at the end of the corridor. "Jessie? Who's Priscilla Parsons?"

He waited, but she was gone now and for a moment Garrett stood all alone at the station. He began to look around, and suddenly all the shadows in the corners seemed a little more menacing.

"Damn it, I'm not that gullible," he continued after a few seconds. "You don't get me that easily."

***

"Here we go," he muttered a few minutes later, as he entered room thirteen and made his way to the table next to the bed. "I thought I'd change your water. We can't have you drinking old water, can we?"

He set the bottle down, before forcing himself to look at the figure in the bed. Something about the sight of Tommy Wallace left him feeling distinctly uneasy. Now that he was stable, Tommy had been left sedated on the bed, with thick bandages covering his face; Garrett had been part of the team that had treated him when he'd first arrived at the hospital, and as he stared at the bandages he knew full well that the poor man's eyes had been ripped right out of their sockets. In truth, most of the team had assumed that Tommy was on the way out, but he'd managed to pull through and now he was hooked up to various machines. Although he knew that most likely Tommy couldn't hear him right now, Garrett figured that he still needed to be polite.

"Well, you might not be drinking this water at the moment," he continued uncertainly, as Tommy remained flat on his back in the bed, "but it's nice to have it. I'll be back in an hour or two to check on you again, and then Doctor Toscarini'll come in the morning and decide what to do with you."

He hesitated, and then he turned to head out of the room. As he reached the door, however, he stopped as he heard the bed creaking. He froze for a moment, reminding himself that the patient was far too heavily sedated to wake up, but already he could feel the hairs standing up on the back of his neck.

Finally, slowly, he turned to see that Tommy was now sitting up in the bed, looking directly toward him despite the bandages covering his eye sockets.

"Uh... hey," Garrett said cautiously, already wondering exactly who he should call about this development. "Dude, just hold on for a moment and I'll fetch -"

"She's coming," Tommy said suddenly, cutting him off.

"I beg your pardon?"

"No," Tommy continued, his voice sounding strangely flat and emotionless, "she's already here."

"I don't quite know what you mean," Garrett replied, "but -"

"I tried so hard to keep the two worlds separate," Tommy added, interrupting him yet again, "but now I see that I was a fool all along. Everything I did was in vain, because they will always find a way to cross over."

"Right," Garrett said, furrowing his brow. "Okay, but I really think I should call someone."

"They can't say I didn't warn them," Tommy said, "or that I didn't try. I did everything in my power, but those boys wouldn't listen. The three of them were always so stubborn, so set in their ways, and I knew that eventually I'd be unable to control them. Twenty years have passed since I left this world, and I think the time has come for me to stop looking over them all. They can deal with this mess themselves. They showed that they have no loyalty to me, so why should I have loyalty to them? Especially when I can already feel Sangreth calling me away."

"Um..."

For a moment, Garrett really had no idea how to respond.

"Okay," he added finally. "That's cool, but I'm still gonna go and fetch someone."

"I shall move on to Sangreth," Tommy – or

rather, the voice speaking through him – continued, "and leave those boys to settle their grievances with one another down here in the mud. They never listened to my advice anyway, even long before the Interferer, and I see no reason to waste more of my breath. Tradition dictates that a father should always wait around and watch over his sons after death, and before retiring to Sangreth, but twenty years is long enough. My work here is done. And if those boys bring everything crashing to the ground... I can at least say that I did my best."

"Right," Garrett said, before swallowing hard. "That's absolutely brilliant. I'm just going to go and make a couple of calls and see if I can get someone to come and check you over." He waited for an answer, but he felt increasingly unnerved as Tommy merely continued to stare blindly in his direction. "Okay?"

Again, he waited.

"Okay," he added, turning to leave. "I'll be -"

Suddenly Tommy let out a pained gasp and fell back against the bed, convulsing frantically as if every nerve in his body was firing all at once. As the machines began to emit their various alarms and warnings, Garrett raced over to the bed and looked down at Tommy's face, and he saw thick spittle already spraying from the man's lips. A moment later Jessie ran through and stopped on the other side of the bed, and then she grabbed the cart from the corner of the room and rolled it over.

"What's happening to him?" Garrett stammered.

"I don't know, but he's gonna rip himself apart," she replied, already pulling out various items of equipment. "Don't just stand there, Garrett! We have to do something!"

CHAPTER ELEVEN

Twenty years earlier...

"MICHAEL, YOU'RE SCARING ME."

"I'm scaring myself too," he replied, still staring out the window, watching as the two wolves maintained their patrol in the clearing in front of the cabin.

"Can we just put our cards on the table?" she asked with a sigh. "I'm *so* sick of the half-answers you give me to all my questions. You mentioned your father just now, but where is he? And who is he? I know so little about you, and I don't think that's got anything to do with my memory problems. Did I ever know where you come from?"

"You're so beautiful," he said, turning to her

suddenly.

"Michael -"

"You've aged," he added before she could get another word out. "Don't get me wrong, I can see the years on your face. The lines. The stress." He stepped closer and put a hand on the side of her cheek, as if to hold her still so that he could inspect her features more closely. "How old are you now?"

"I..."

She hesitated for a moment, before realizing – as the candle continued to flicker on the sill nearby – that playing along was most likely her only way to get any answers at all.

"Forties," she told him finally. "Don't ask a lady to be more specific."

"I love what time has done to you," he continued. "I love the way it's... sculpted your features and made them more pronounced."

"Thanks," she replied cautiously. "I think."

"Your eyes are deeper," he added. "There's more pain in them. Life hasn't been easy, but you're still strong. I'm sorry, you have to forgive me, this is the first time I've been truly close to you in so very long. Your scent has changed subtly but it's still so very you."

"And you *haven't* changed," she replied. "Not one bit. How is that even possible, or is it something to do with the whole... wolf thing?"

"You must have a lot of questions."

"After I saw you turning into a wolf? Yeah, kind of."

"I come from a family that has lived in this forest for centuries," he continued. "We were here long before humans settled in the area, and we'll be here long after humans are gone. Well, that's what the others always say, but I've never been quite so sure. I don't think humans ever really go away once they arrive in a place, and it's not like the town has been showing signs of getting any smaller. There's a delicate balance between the two worlds, but for a while now the humans have been encroaching on our territory more and more. Then, recently, those power lines went up."

"What power lines?"

"The ones that run through the forest."

"Those aren't recent," she pointed out. "They've been there for decades now."

"You don't consider that recent?" He hesitated for a moment, as if he was a little confused. "That's right, you see time a little differently. The point is, some in our world saw that power lines as an act of war. It's not just the lines themselves, or the pylons. It's more than that. It's the buzz in the air that stretches for miles, and it's the charge that we can all feel whenever we go anywhere near those things. That was supposed to be our territory, but one day the humans just tore through the forest and built those monstrosities. And now are you really surprised that we're angry?"

"Is that what this is all about?" she asked. "The power line?"

"We should have known your people would show no respect," he continued. "I mean, you even built a railroad through your own cemetery. You kind of have a history of cutting into sacred things."

"But what does all of this have to do with us?" she asked, trying once again to get to the root of the problem. "I still don't understand why those wolves are so angry." She reached out and touched the side of his arm, only for him to wince and pull back. "You're in pain."

"It's nothing."

"It's because you've been in your human form for so long," she reminded him, still shocked that such crazy words were leaving her lips at all. "You admitted it yourself, Michael. You need to turn back."

He shook his head.

"Why not?"

"Because of how you looked at me," he replied.

"That's because I didn't understand," she continued. "I was scared, and I was in shock, and I wasn't prepared for my boyfriend to suddenly start turning into a wolf." She paused, seeing the pain and fear in his bloodied eyes. "But I get it now," she added cautiously, "and I think I understand, so I won't react the same way."

"I'm fine like this."

"You're clearly *not* fine."

"I can live with it," he continued, even as more flakes of dead skin fell from around his lips, revealing the reddened patches beneath. "Eventually I'll find a way to stabilize it, Lisa, but I refuse to turn into one of those things ever again. I swore twenty years ago that it wouldn't happen, and I didn't wait all this time just to succumb now. Not when you're right in front of me again."

"I want you to be what you're supposed to be," she told him. "That's so clearly not what you are now."

He shook his head again.

"Try it," she replied. "Just once, change again and see how I react. I swear I won't scream, and I won't faint or anything like that. I *want* to see you in your natural form."

"You really don't."

"Trust me," she said firmly.

"You're sweet for saying this," he told her, shivering slightly as if the effort of retaining his form was almost too much, "but you have no idea what you'd be letting yourself in for. It's not only my body that'd change, it's also my mind. I'd still be me, but other instincts would come to the fore. I don't know if I can trust myself."

"*I* trust you," she replied. "Isn't that

enough?"

She waited, and this time she began to hope that perhaps she was getting through to him. He looked around the room, almost as if he was contemplating his options, and when he turned to her again something seemed to have softened in his eyes. He opened his mouth, poised to say something, and after a few seconds the shivering stopped. And then, as a wolf howled outside the cabin, he turned and looked at the window.

"Ignore them," Lisa said.

"I can't."

"Michael -"

"You don't understand," he continued, and now he seemed to be almost shaking with rage. "Years ago, I thought that if I came out here, they'd leave me alone eventually. I thought they'd understand that I didn't want anything to do with that world, that I only wanted to be alone, but they've never accepted that. Now they blame me for what's happening, they even put up that stupid gate in a pathetic attempt to draw a line in the sand, but they're incapable of seeing the world the way it really is. Even now, he thinks he can show up here and put everything right." He paused for a moment before clenching his fists. "I hate him."

"Do you mean your father?" Lisa asked.

"He's got two other sons," he replied through gritted teeth, still watching the window as wolves continued to howl outside. "That should be enough. He doesn't even need me."

"Yes, but -"

"But nothing!" he shouted angrily, turning to her as more wolves howled in the clearing. "This is exactly what I was trying to make you see, Lisa! This is a world that you can't possibly understand, and the really dangerous thing is that you think it's within your grasp when it's not! You're the smartest person I've ever met, but that doesn't mean anything out here! Do you have any idea how hard it is to resist him? He always gets what he wants, no matter what! Nothing can hurt him, even silver bullets barely slow him down. If any of the rest of us took a silver bullet in the right spot, we'd be done for, but for him it's be barely a scratch. There's only one thing that can truly stop him, and that's..."

His voice trailed off for a few more seconds.

"He thinks he's completely safe for all threats," he added darkly. "He thinks no-one else in the whole world can send him to Sangreth. Sometimes I think he's overdue for a lesson."

Hearing more and more wolves howling outside, Lisa stepped past Michael and made her way back to the window. Looking out into the clearing, she was shocked to see that a dozen or more wolves had gathered now, with more emerging from the darkness of the forest. And then, before she had a chance to ask Michael what they all wanted, she spotted something else stepping out from between the trees, something she could barely believe she was seeing. Yet another wolf had arrived, but this one was almost double the size of all the others, walking slowly and steadily with such force that Lisa couldn't help thinking that the ground must be shaking beneath its paws.

"Michael?" she said finally, her voice trembling with fear. "I could be wrong, but I think your dad might be here now."

CHAPTER TWELVE

Today...

STILL PICKING HIS WAY through the forest several hours after he'd set off from the road, John had to duck down in an attempt to get past a particularly low hanging branch. Finding that his path was almost entirely blocked by branches, he twisted first one way and then the other, finally managing to clamber over some fallen logs until he stopped for a moment to get his breath back.

Looking up, he saw an almost full moon hanging in the sky high above.

"I would suggest that you pay attention to your instincts," he remembered the ghost of Amanda Mathis telling him, "and to your dreams, and to the things that you're not sure you're really seeing. You'll find the answers you seek, but you don't have all the time in the world. You need to find her before the next full moon."

"Find her?" he'd replied, thinking that she meant Little Miss Dead back at the station. "Finding her's not the problem."

"I'm not necessarily talking about the girl," Amanda had told him, "although they're not entirely unconnected. This is the last time I'll be able to speak to you in this way. Next time... I might be considerably more terrified."

"Thanks for that," he muttered now. "Real useful."

He watched the moon for a few more seconds before looking around again. He shone his flashlight between two nearby trees, not because of any sound but simply because he wanted to make absolutely sure he was alone; he turned and looked the other way, but the silence of the forest seemed almost to be reaching out to him until finally he realized that he could hear a faint whistling sound coming from nearby, accompanied by a low and slightly irregular rattle.

Worried that he might have taken the wrong path, John began to try to follow the whistling sound, and after just a few more minutes he emerged at the edge of a familiar clearing. On the other side he saw the trees that had once been decorated with the bones of men who'd died in the bus crash twenty years earlier; those bones, including the skulls, were long gone now but somehow in that moment John felt sure that he could once again hear the wind howling through the skulls. The more he listened, the more the voices became clearer.

"You're going the wrong way," one of the voices seemed almost to be saying. "You don't belong here."

Looking down at the ground nearby, John realized that he was at the spot where Joe Hicks had been torn apart by wolves. He felt a shiver run through his bones, and he half-expected to see Joe's grinning ghost watching from nearby, although he quickly told himself that would be one horrific development too many.

"He is gone now," another voice whispered above, even though the skulls were gone. "He has journeyed to Sangreth. Those who are left behind must deal with his passing."

"What are you talking about?" John asked, even though he wasn't even sure that the voices were real. "What's Sangreth?"

"You will know," the first voice replied, "when you too set foot upon its hallowed ground. Sangreth is waiting for you, as it has waited for so many before. And you shall have no choice. You must answer its call in the end."

John waited, but the wind had begun to die

down now and after a few more seconds he realized that the voices seemed to have stopped. A shiver passed through his bones, and already he was trying to untangle the knot of confused meaning in the words he'd heard. He had no idea who or what Sangreth was supposed to be, or where it was supposed to be waiting, and finally he figured that perhaps he was letting his imagination run a little too wild.

Reaching into his pocket, he pulled out his phone and checked yet again for some kind of signal. Seeing that he had no bars at all, he slipped the phone away, and then he turned just in time to spot something moving in the forest nearby. He froze, and sure enough a moment later he saw the one-eyed wolf slipping past some trees in the moonlight.

Slowly, John reached down for his gun.

***

"I didn't know any better," Robert Law said, sitting on the floor in his office with his back against the bookshelf he'd pulled across the door. "All I knew was that Lisa was another patient, somehow I never joined the dots and connected her to Sobolton until it was too late. Truth be told, I probably barely even noticed her name on the patient sheet at all. If I did, it certainly didn't register with me."

He paused for a moment, thinking back to that terrible day many years earlier when he'd met Rod Sondnes and had first made the connection to Lisa.

"For me," he continued, "Lisa Sondnes was just another patient shunted over to me by that idiot Campbell. He was murdered by a patient years later, by the way, shortly before Lakehurst burned to the ground. I'd never wish harm on anyone, but I have to admit that I didn't shed any tears when I heard the news. Once I realized that Lisa was here, I made sure to keep out of her way. That wasn't easy, and eventually she spotted me in the street, but I honestly think she didn't recognize me at all. That entire part of her memory had been burned away."

Staring straight ahead across the darkened office, he thought back to the moment when he'd first turned the dial up to the maximum setting, delivering a shock to Lisa's brain that he'd always known was too great.

"I was just following orders," he added, with tears in his eyes. "I always did exactly what Doctor Campbell wanted, and I never asked questions. Then, after a while, I heard about her disappearance and I couldn't help but wonder whether I had anything to do with it. I didn't want to admit what had happened, of course, so I simply tried to get the truth out of Joe Hicks. Damn it, I never liked that little bastard, but eventually I came to believe him when he told me that he didn't know the truth. And when he told me to stop worrying, that Lisa was gone forever, eventually I came to believe him, even if deep down..."

He took a deep breath.

"Deep down I always felt that Joe knew more than he was letting on. I said just now that I believed him, but that was another lie. Joe always dropped these little hints that he knew something about the forest, that he had some inkling of whatever was out there. The first clue was when the bus crash happened and Joe went to great lengths to cover it all up. I knew there was something out there, but I didn't want to open that can of worms and find out for myself. I don't know whether that makes me a bad person, although in truth I'm fairly sure I became a bad person back when I worked at Lakehurst. And when Lisa Sondnes vanished, it was like a miracle. The one reminder of my time there, in my daily life, was suddenly gone."

Leaning back, he struggled to hold back more tears.

"The tangled webs of a liar, huh?" he added. "I told myself that I was doing good work at Lakehurst, that the good outweighed the bad. I quit not long after Lisa's case, and my life has been a mess ever since. The guilt has been eating away at me, though, and tonight I think it's going to make me pay. That's what you're here for, isn't it? You're here to make me suffer for what I did. Well..."

He paused, before getting to his feet and slowly sliding the bookcase away from the door.

"I'm done hiding," he continued, reaching for the handle, preparing to face the little girl on the other side. "I don't know why you look like her, or how, but you're obviously here to punish me. I suppose you might have been sent by God or..."

His voice trailed off.

"It's funny," he added, "but when people ask me whether I believe in God and all that stuff, I've always found it easy to tell them that I don't. It's only now, facing my fate, that I realize I was wrong all that time. I believe in all of it, but I couldn't admit that to myself, and now I think I understand why I have to pay for my sins." Slowly, he turned the handle and pulled the door open. "Whatever my punishment is going to be," he added, with fresh tears in his eyes, "I -"

Before he could finish, he saw that there was nobody standing on the other side of the door. He limped forward and looked both ways along the corridor, but there was no sign of anyone at all. He'd been talking for a good few minutes now, and he'd assumed that the girl was listening, yet evidently at some point she'd simply wandered away.

"Hello?" he called out. "Little girl? Eloise? Lisa? Is anyone there?"

CHAPTER THIRTEEN

Twenty years earlier...

"KEEP THE DOOR LOCKED," Michael said as he stepped out through the cabin's front door. "Whatever you do, don't come out here until they're gone. Do you understand me, Lisa?"

"I understand, but -"

"So shut the door," he said firmly, turning to her as the wolves continued to gather in the clearing. "I mean it. No more questions, at least not for now. I have to face them alone."

"Isn't there *anything* I can do?" she asked, struggling to hold back tears.

He shook his head.

"Are they going to try to hurt you?" she continued.

"Hopefully not," he said firmly. "If my brothers were here alone, then maybe, but with my father here as well... I've got a feeling that this is going to be more of a formal encounter. I just have to hope that I can make him understand once and for all." He hesitated for a moment, before suddenly stepping back over to her. "You shouldn't be here," he told her, "but now that you are, I'm going to defend you. I think I know how, there's one thing I can do, I... I don't want to do it, but it's a last resort. And for you... Lisa, there's nothing I wouldn't do to protect you."

"You're kinda scaring me," she told him, before looking across the clearing and seeing the gathered wolves. "Actually, I think they're the ones doing the scaring. You're more... worrying me deeply."

"Wait inside, and hopefully this will all be okay," he told her, "but if it's not... Lisa, I don't want you to ever forget how I feel about you. Do you promise?"

"Second time lucky," she suggested cautiously.

"Now wait inside," he added, pushing her back. "When I -"

Suddenly she stepped forward and kissed him, and the kiss lasted for several seconds until finally she pulled back and looked up into his eyes.

"I've only just found you again," she

whispered, reaching down and squeezing his hand tight. "Please, Michael, I don't want to lose you. Not now. Not ever."

She waited, hoping that he'd tell her how everything was going to be alright, but instead he simply looked into her eyes for a moment longer before stepping back. He seemed on the verge of saying something, until finally he turned and stepped away; as soon as he was outside, he pulled the cabin's door shut, and Lisa immediately hurried to the window so she could watch as he walked down the steps and out into the moonlit clearing. Already, she could feel her chest tightening with fear as she saw that most of the wolves had formed a kind of semicircle around the clearing's edge, while the larger wolf appeared to be simply waiting as Michael made his way closer. Although Michael certainly seemed to know what he was doing, Lisa still worried that he was putting himself in great danger.

A moment later she hurried to the corner of the room and grabbed her rifle. Once she was back at the window, with the silver shot loaded, she saw that Michael was still merely standing in front of the large wolf, and she couldn't shake the feeling that somehow they were quietly communicating.

***

"I never asked for any of this," Michael said, standing out in the clearing as a cold wind blew across the clearing, ruffling the wolf's fur as well as his own clothes. "All I ever wanted was to be left alone."

He waited, staring into the large wolf's dark eyes, and a moment later a shudder passed through his chest.

"I know," he continued, before holding his hands up and looking at the ravaged, bloodied skin, "but it's a price I'm willing to pay. When she saw my other form, she -"

He stopped suddenly, as if interrupted by a voice he could hear only in his head.

"I know that," he added, sounding a little more frustrated now, "but you have to understand that I have no choice. I never intended to meet anyone else, certainly not someone from the town, but it happened and now..."

His voice trailed off as he tried to work out exactly how to explain.

"This doesn't have to change anything," he said cautiously, still looking at his own damaged hands. "I know there are two worlds balanced here, but we want to exist outside them both. There's even a chance... I know she wants to go away, and if I were to go with her, then why would any of this have to be a problem?"

As it to answer that question, one of the

nearby wolves growled. Michael turned and saw that the wolf with one eye had edged a little closer.

"How could *you* ever hoped to understand?" he asked, unable to hide a sense of bitterness. "You don't know anything about love. All you know about is hatred and fear."

Now it was the larger wolf's turn to growl, and Michael turned to see its eyes narrowing slightly.

"You know I'm right, Father," he continued. "You also know that I have every right to choose my own path. Wouldn't it actually make things easier for all of us if I just... removed myself from the situation? That'd mean one less son for you to worry about. You had three, but if I leave then you'll be down to just one. Let him take the lead. I'm sure he'll be a disaster, but perhaps the others will eventually take matters into their own hands."

He heard another growling sound; turning, he saw that the one-eyed wolf had edged even closer. A moment later the larger wolf growled again, causing the other wolf to pull back a little.

"I know you worry about the future," Michael said, turning to the larger wolf again, "but you can't guarantee that things will be alright. Face it, none of your sons can live up to your legacy, so you're just going to have to let go and accept that we'll work things out after you're gone."

The large wolf snarled again, and this time

thick saliva began to drip from its jaw. Huge, sharp teeth glinted in the moonlight.

"That's what this is really about, isn't it?" Michael added. "You're old, Father, and you know that your time has to end eventually. Are you preparing for that moment now? What if -"

He flinched suddenly, as if he'd heard something in his mind that brought genuine pain.

"Get angry all you like," he sneered, "but that only proves that I'm speaking the truth. And here's some more truth for you... I don't want any part of this. I don't care what happens to our pack, or to this stupid little town they call Sobolton, or to the forest or any of it. Instead of getting drawn into it like the rest of the family, I just wanted to pretend none of it exists. I used to think I could do that by pulling away and living out here alone, but now I finally understand that I have to go even further than that. I have to go so far away that you never even sense my lifeblood again." He paused. "Fine. I'm willing to make that sacrifice because -"

He flinched again.

"Yes, of course I love her!" he snapped angrily. "Does that disgust you? And I know I can't stay looking like this forever, but I'll... I'll find a way to make it work. I'll do anything it takes to find a way to live with Lisa. I'm not asking you to like her, and I'm not asking you to accept her. I'm just asking you to let us go, because if you don't..."

He reached slowly toward his pocket, but at the last second he held back.

"You're a lot of things, Father," he added, struggling to stay calm, "but I've never mistaken you for an idiot. You once taught me to look past my emotions and see the truth. Isn't it about time that you did that?"

Expecting to hear another growl from the one-eyed wolf, he turned to his left, only to see that the wolf was gone. Trying not to panic, he turned and saw to his horror that the creature had been silently edging closer to the front of the cabin.

"Hey!" he yelled, hurrying across the clearing and stepping in front of the wolf before it could reach the steps. "What are you doing?" he asked, looking down into the wolf's one good eye. "I should've known this was all just a trick. You came to distract me so you could finish her off!"

The one-eyed wolf snarled, but Michael immediately kicked it hard in the side, forcing it back.

"Don't make excuses, Father!" he continued, keeping his eyes fixed on the creature as it snarled at him again. "Maybe you were all in on the plan or maybe you weren't, but we both know he can't be trusted. He's always been the one who -"

Before he could finish, the one-eyed wolf lunged at him, biting his arm and dragging him down onto the ground. Letting out a cry of pain,

Michael tried to pull free, but already the wolf's teeth were tearing through his flesh.

"Father, tell him to stop!" Michael shouted, kicking the beast hard in the flank but not managing to push it away. "Father, make -"

Suddenly a shot rang out and the one-eyed wolf yelped, pulling back in agony. Already blood was gushing from a wound on its flank, and the wolf whimpered again, struggling to stay up as it tried frantically to limp away. Horrified, Michael stared for a moment before turning to see Lisa standing in the cabin's open doorway, holding a smoking rifle.

"Get inside!" she said firmly, keeping her eyes fixed firmly on the larger wolf in the center of the clearing. "That was my last silver shot. Something tells me a few more would be useful right about now."

CHAPTER FOURTEEN

Today...

SLIPPING BETWEEN TWO MORE trees in the darkness, still holding his gun in his right hand, John tried to make as little noise as possible as he edged his way through the forest. He hadn't seen the one-eyed wolf for a couple of minutes now, but somehow he felt certain that the creature was watching him from somewhere nearby, almost as if -

Suddenly hearing a cracking sound, he spun and held the gun up. He almost fired, only to hold back at the very last second as he realized that he'd just be wasting one of the silver bullets.

"I saw you earlier," he whispered, adjusting his grip on the gun. "All I need is one good shot..."

For a moment he thought back to the horrific sight of the wolves tearing Joe Hicks apart. He knew that this wolf had been involved in the attack, which meant that there was no question about its level of threat; unable to shake the sense that he was being tracked through the forest, John told himself that he might only get one shot if the wolf attacked. He waited for a few more seconds, and then he turned and looked the other way. Despite the cold night air, he could already feel himself starting to sweat.

"Right between the eyes," he continued. "That's where I'll get you. I'm not -"

Before he could finish, he heard another cracking sound. He turned and looked the other way, and this time he was just in time to spot the wolf racing past some nearby trees. Raising his gun, John fired, but he succeeded only in hitting one of the trees, and the wolf had already vanished from sight. For a few seconds, John could hear the sound of the animal hurrying again, before the forest fell silent once again.

"Damn it," he muttered, fully aware that he'd missed and – in the process – wasted one of the silver bullets. That meant he was down to just five. "I won't be missing again."

After a couple more minutes, he began to set off again, still trying to maintain at least some sense of his surroundings. He had a vague idea which way he was going, and the moon above was casting an ethereal silver glow that at least helped him find his way; reaching out, he steadied himself against one of the trees as he made his way past, but he knew he wasn't exactly being very stealthy. Any wolf with semi-decent hearing would be able to locate him from a mile off, and he also worried that this particular wolf might not be acting alone. There could be any number of -

In that moment he heard a cracking sound again, this time coming from somewhere over his shoulder. He turned and saw the one-eyed wolf staring back at him; raising the gun, John fired again, hitting one of the trees as the wolf raced away once more into the darkness.

"Damn it, what -"

"He's toying with you."

Startled, John spun around and raised the gun again. His heart was racing, but he saw no sign of anyone else nearby in the forest.

"Who's there?" he called out, before reminding himself that he needed to keep from showing fear. "My name is John Tench and I'm with the -"

"I know who you are," the voice said, interrupting him, still seemingly coming from nowhere and everywhere all at once. "I've made it my business to know. You have to understand that the wolf only has one intention right now, and that's to make you waste all your silver bullets. Once you've done that, you'll be defenseless and he can pick you off at his leisure." He paused for a moment. "How many do you have left, anyway? Five? Four?"

"I need you to come out with your hands up," John replied, "and -"

"I'm not going to do that."

"You really don't have a choice."

"Of course I have a choice," the voice continued. "Come on, deep down you must realize that you're far beyond your territory now. This place simply isn't part of your jurisdiction, not really. You made a mistake coming out here tonight, but that mistake doesn't have to be fatal."

"Come out so that I can see you."

"I'd really rather not."

"Then -"

"You're going to do something for me," the voice added, cutting him off yet again.

"And why would I do that, when I haven't even seen your face?" John asked.

"Because you're a smart man," the voice replied, and now John was starting to realize that it seemed to be coming from somewhere slightly to his left. "Because even in your short amount of time here in Sobolton, you must have realized that this place is unlike anywhere else you've ever been before. I get it, you're used to uncovering the truth and straightening things out, but that's not how things work here. Not in the town, and certainly not in the forest. Your predecessor, for all his many faults, at least understood that fact."

Hearing yet another cracking sound, John looked over his shoulder.

"Relax," the voice continued, "he won't come for you right now. Not when I'm here and, besides, he knows you've still got silver bullets. He's been shot by one of those before and he barely survived. He won't make the same mistake again."

"You seem to know a lot about the forest," John continued, looking to his left as he played for time and tried to spot the other man in the moonlight. "Have we met before?"

"Yes and no."

"What does that mean?"

"It means that the answer to your question doesn't matter," the voice said firmly. "What matters is that you give me what I want. She doesn't have to be hidden or protected from me, not when I'm... Well, there's really no need for you to know about any of that. I want you to bring her to me."

"Who are you talking about?"

"I'm talking about the girl. I'm talking about Eloise."

"How do you know her?"

"I considered taking her by force," the voice explained, "but that has never quite worked out too

123

well for me in the past. I want to be smarter now. I want you to bring her to me, so that she can make the choice herself to come to me. I want her to understand that she has no reason to be afraid."

"You're talking about her as if she's..."

John's voice trailed off for a moment as he weighed up whether or not to reveal the truth. Finally he figured that he needed to try to unsettle the other man somehow, so he resolved to tell the truth.

"I'm sorry to have to tell you this," he continued finally, "but Eloise is dead. We found her body in the frozen lake, and she's been in the morgue ever since. We've been struggling to find out much about her, though so if you..."

Realizing that he could hear the voice chuckling slightly, John hesitated.

"Is something funny?" he asked.

"Just your narrow little way of seeing the world," the voice replied. "I'm fully aware of what's been going on in your silly little town. I've been watching it all, more or less. You think Eloise is dead, and that's perfectly understandable, but I promise you that right now she's up and about. There are people in this world who think she needs to be protected from me. They have their reasons, but they're wrong and the time has come for the games to end. If you're smart, Sheriff John Tench, you'll go back to the town and fetch Eloise, and you'll bring her to me so that I can persuade her to return. And then you'll go back to your desk in your office, and you'll fake some paperwork to cover your tracks, and you'll pretend that none of this happened."

"I'm afraid I can't do that," John told him.

"Of course you can," the voice said. "Mr. Hicks was most amenable in these matters. He did more or less everything I ever asked of him. He even kept Lisa's apartment exactly as it was when she was last in there, so that it'd be ready when..." He hesitated again. "You're doing it again. You have a way of tricking me into almost saying too much, but I really have to watch myself. Do we have a deal, Mr. Tench? Are you going to fetch Eloise and bring her to meet me in say... one hour?"

"Let me see you."

"You've already -"

"Are you the one who attacked my deputy tonight?" John asked, feeling a growing sense of anger in his chest. "He's a good man and he's fighting for his life right now at the hospital. Are you the one who put him there?"

"Of course I am," the voice replied, "and you should take that as a warning. My father's spirit is still here, but not for long. Once he's gone, there'll be a vacuum in the power balance and I realize now that I have to take my rightful place. I once wanted to run away and leave this place behind forever, but now I see that there's only one way I can ever keep my family safe. After all, they say that attack is the best form of defense."

"I need to take you to the station and ask you a whole lot of questions," John said firmly, struggling to contain his fury as he thought of Tommy's bloodied figure back in the hospital. "That's not a request, it's an order. Do you understand?"

He waited, but he heard no response.

"Do you understand?" he asked again, worried that the voice might be gone. "Say something! I need -"

Suddenly an arm wrapped around his throat from behind, quickly pulling tight and forcing John onto his knees as the gun slipped from his hand.

"I'm done trying to do this the nice way!" Michael sneered, leaning down to look into John's shocked face. "I've told you what I want, and I want it now! Are you going to give it to me, or am I going to have to kill you and come up with a better plan?"

CHAPTER FIFTEEN

Twenty years earlier...

"GET BACK INSIDE!" MICHAEL shouted, stumbling to his feet. "Lisa, are you insane? I told you to wait in there!"

"I'll go inside when you come with me," she stammered, her voice filled with fear as she kept the rifle raised and watched the injured one-eyed wolf limped away past the edge of the clearing. "I don't know what's going on here, Michael, but -"

"That's exactly the point!" he snarled, stepping toward her. "You don't have a clue! I can handle this, I can talk my father round, but first you have to give me a chance!"

"Your father?" she replied, before looking over at the large wolf in the center of the clearing.

"Is that... I mean, is he... that wolf, is it *really* your..."

Her voice trailed off, and for a moment she felt as if she couldn't possibly complete that thought. After a few seconds, however, she raised the rifle and aimed at the large wolf. Silver shots or no silver shots, she figured she could at least slow the creature down.

"Put that down," Michael said firmly.

She shook her head.

"It's not as if it can hurt him," he continued. "All you'll do is annoy him, and believe me, he already doesn't like you very much. That's both my brothers you've shot now."

"What are you talking about?"

"Lisa, I need you to help me calm this situation down," he said, stepping toward her and slowly reaching out as if he meant to take the gun from her hands. Sure enough, that's exactly what he tried, only for her to strengthen her grip in defiance. "Lisa, I know you mean well," he continued, "but you're messing with someone you don't understand."

"What do they want from you?" she asked, as she saw the other wolves slowly starting to stalk closer. "Michael, now's the time to tell me exactly what's going on."

"You shot my brother," he replied.

"Your... if you mean the wolf with one eye,

then I had no choice!"

"Not just him," he explained. "I had two brothers, and the other one was shot recently while he was trying to rescue his cubs. He's out there in the forest now, alone and terrified, trapped halfway between his wolf and human forms. That's because of the silver bullet you fired, but he won't let anyone get close enough to help him."

"I didn't know," she replied. "How could I have known?"

"Our father senses that his time is drawn to a close," he continued. "When that happens, there are two stages. First the physical body dies, and then the soul leaves after a few more years. He wants to get the succession plan in place before he goes, but that's all been thrown into disarray. Deep down, I know he wants me to take his place, but I refuse. I never wanted that, not even before I met you. And now, I just want us to get away from here forever and never look back."

"We can do that," she told him, shocked by the words that were leaving her own mouth. "I don't know how, I don't know where we'll go but... Michael, now that I remember you, I'm not going to let you go again."

"It's not that simple," he told her as the wolves edged closer still. "There are certain... traditions that have to be respected. At least, that's what my father and the others think. They also don't think that it's right for me to fraternize with someone from the town, they think you're a danger."

"Then I'll prove them wrong," she replied, before pushing past him and stepping toward the large wolf in the middle of the clearing. "I don't know how, but I'll make them see sense."

"Lisa! Don't!" Michael called after her.

"Can he understand me?" she asked as she stopped in front of the large wolf and saw his dark eyes staring back at her. "Does he know what I'm saying?"

"He knows," Michael replied, and now his voice was trembling with fear.

"Then I want him to know that I didn't ask to be in the middle of all this," she continued, making sure to maintain eye contact with the large wolf even though every fiber in her being was telling her to run. "I want him to know that I never meant to cause any trouble, that I was only trying to live my life without getting in anyone's way. It's not my fault that I..." Her voice trailed off for a moment. "It's not my fault," she added finally, "that I fell in love with someone who's not from the town. And I know it took twenty years, but I remembered it all eventually. Doesn't that prove something? Doesn't it show that whatever we're feeling has to be real? It's almost like it's... supposed to be like this."

"Lisa, come over here," Michael replied, reaching a hand out toward her. "Now! I'm not kidding, you have no idea how much danger you're in right now."

"Maybe that's the point," she said, before leaning down and setting the rifle on the ground, then standing tall again. Her hands were shaking with fear, but she didn't mind letting that show now. "Maybe I have to show them that I'm not going to run away."

"Lisa -"

"Because I'm not," she added, with tears in her eyes now as she somehow managed to keep her gaze fixed on the large wolf. "Have we met before?"

"Lisa, please just -"

"Have we met before?" she asked again. "If this is your father... have I met him and forgotten?"

"No, but -"

"So I get it," she continued, clenching and then unclenching her fists. "He probably thinks I'm some weak little person who can't possibly fit into your world, and he might be right but... doesn't it count for something that I'm willing to try?"

"Lisa," Michael replied, "listen to me very carefully. You need to slowly move away and come toward me. Don't turn your back on him, just come this way and I'll get you safely into the cabin."

"I didn't feel very safe in there before," she

told him, before taking a deep breath. "If he can understand me, then I want him to know that I'm not going anywhere. I know I left you before, but that wasn't my fault, I was dragged away by Joe Hicks and by my father. I won't let that happen again, but somehow I found a way to remember and that has to count for something, right?"

"Lisa, step away from him," Michael said firmly.

She hesitated, before forcing herself to instead take a step forward.

"You're out of your mind!" Michael hissed.

"Hi," she said, close enough to the large wolf now to almost reach out and touch him. "We haven't met properly, but my name is Lisa Sondnes and I'm from Sobolton." She swallowed hard. "I guess you probably already know that. Anyway, I met your son twenty years ago but then all my memories of that time were kinda... zapped out of my head. It took a long time for me to get them back, and I'm not even sure if I've got *all* of them yet, but I'm standing here now and I'm not leaving without him." She paused again, terrified that she might say something wrong yet also determined to get through to the creature. "The truth is," she added, "I love him."

In that moment, she realized that she meant those three words with every ounce of her soul. A flicker of shock ran through her chest, as if she could barely believe that she felt that way, and she couldn't help but worry that she sounded like one of those heroines in the romance novels she'd read as a kid. At the same time, she also felt a strange kind of strength that she knew could only come from speaking the truth.

Slowly, the large wolf bared its fangs and let out a low, rumbling growl. Lisa wasn't sure whether the ground was actually starting to rumble, or whether that sensation was all in her head.

"So maybe you hate that fact," she continued. "Maybe you hate *me*. All I'm asking is for a chance to prove myself, because I happen to think that your son's pretty great. And I'm sorry if I hurt your other son, or more than one of them, but that was a mistake. I'll try to put everything right as best I can. I'm a veterinarian, actually, so I might actually have a shot at helping." She slowly reached out with her right hand, determined to show the large wolf that she wanted to be a friend. "Can you see past everything else?" she asked. "Can you try to understand what I'm saying to you?"

"Lisa," Michael said cautiously, "you need to get away from him right now."

"No, I think it's working," she replied, before turning to him and managing a faint smile. "I think -"

"Lisa!"

In that moment Lisa saw the absolute terror

in Michael's eyes. Before she had a chance to react, however, a huge weight slammed against her from behind, throwing her down to the ground and landing on top of her as she heard a horrifyingly loud roar filling her ears.

CHAPTER SIXTEEN

Today...

"YOU'RE MAKING A MISTAKE!" John hissed, struggling to get free as Michael continued to hold him down on his knees from behind, with one arm wrapped tight against his throat. "I'm an officer of the law and -"

"Not *my* law!" Michael snarled, spitting hot breath at the side of John's face. "Not out here. Don't you get it? That's been the point all along. Your law doesn't apply here. Why can't people from the town ever understand that? Even Lisa thought she knew better."

He hesitated for a moment.

"I'm sorry, Mr. Lawman," he continued, "but your time here's over."

"What happened to Lisa?" John spluttered.

"You wouldn't understand."

"Try me," John said, desperately playing for time as he looked down and tried to work out how he could grab his gun. "You've been to her apartment at least twice recently. You mentioned her just now. What did Lisa Sondnes mean to you?"

"You shouldn't even be saying her name."

"Tell me!"

"Lisa's got nothing to do with you," he sneered.

"She went missing twenty years ago," John replied, trying to perfectly time the moment when he was going to break free and lunge for the gun. "Is she still alive? What did you do to her?"

"Who said *I* did anything to her?" Michael asked.

"But you know who did," John continued, and he was starting to feel that he was making progress. Any mention of Lisa made the other man angry, and John knew that anger would lead to a loss of self-control, and that this would hopefully give him a chance. This was a tactic he'd used many times before, especially back in New York; he'd even used it once against his own son. "You wouldn't believe how many times Lisa's name comes up in my investigations," he explained. "She seems to have been linked to some of the stranger events in Sobolton. If you know anything about her at all, even -"

"Don't say her name!" Michael shouted angrily.

"Why not?"

"Because you just... you don't understand," Michael continued. "I would never have hurt Lisa, I'd have done anything to protect her. Even when they tried to take her away from me and ruin her mind at Lakehurst, I knew I just had to wait and that eventually she'd come back to me. And I was right, too. We were destined to be together and no-one had any right to try to tear us apart. When they did... I made them pay."

"And who are you talking about now?" John asked.

He waited, but he heard no response.

"Who are you talking about?" he said again, before deciding to change his approach. "I'm not sure you've even told me your name," he added. "Can you do that now? I'd at least like to know who I'm talking to."

"I waited so long for her to come back to me," Michael replied, loosening his grip slightly on John's throat, "and then when she did, we only had a short time together before -"

Suddenly John pulled away, taking what he knew would likely be his only chance. He dropped to the ground and grabbed the gun before turning and aiming at Michael; at the last second, however,

Michael let out an angry grunt and ripped the gun from his hands, breaking several of John's fingers in the process before throwing the gun with such force that it broke apart as it slammed against a nearby tree.

Letting out a gasp of pain, John watched as pieces of the gun fell down against the dirt, and then he looked at his hand and saw that three fingers on his right hand were twisted and broken.

"You were just trying to distract me!" Michael said breathlessly. "You don't care about Lisa at all! You were just trying to distract me so you could get away!"

"No!" John shouted, throwing himself across the ground and grabbing parts of the gun, hoping against hope that he might be able to put them together. "I -"

Before he could finish, Michael hauled him up and threw him against one of the other trees. With parts of the gun in his left hand, John winced as he slammed against the trunk, but Michael grabbed him again before he had a chance to slither down to the ground. Looking into Michael's eyes now, John saw nothing but pure anger, and in that moment he finally understood the fury that had left Tommy fighting for his life at the hospital.

Reaching up, John broke a twig from the tree and pushed it into the side of Michael's neck, burying the sharp end deep into the man's damaged flesh. He twisted the twig and pulled it down, tearing the skin, but Michael quickly grabbed his hand and squeezed tight. Feeling more fingers breaking, this time on his left hand, John cried out; he was powerless to resist as Michael moved the hand away and pulled the twig out from his neck.

"Did you think that would stop me?" Michael asked breathlessly, throwing the twig aside as a drop of blood ran down from the wound. "You're even more stupid than I thought."

"I was just... trying to shoot you," John stammered, reaching down with his broken left hand and taking something from his equally broken right hand.

"And how do you think you're going to do that without a gun?" Michael snarled.

"Just a little trick I heard about once," John replied. "Actually, I think it was in a book."

Michael opened his mouth to reply, but at the last second he held back. In that moment, John raised his left hand and slammed it against the side of the man's neck, and he managed to force the silver bullet – which he'd grabbed from the forest floor – straight into the wound he'd made with the twig. He saw the fear in Michael's eyes, but he used that chance to push one of his broken fingers into the side of his neck, forcing the silver bullet deep into Michael's body and already feeling the blood starting to boil and fizz.

Crying out, Michael stumbled back and fell, landing hard on the ground. He reached up and tried to dig the silver bullet out of his neck, but his trembling hands were unable to get close to the wound. John, meanwhile, had slumped down against the side of a nearby tree, struggling to contain the pain from the broken fingers on both hands.

"Let me help you!" John shouted, watching as Michael writhed in agony on the forest's muddy ground. "I can get the bullet out for you, but first you have to agree to help me!"

"Go to Hell!" Michael sobbed, finally managing to dip his fingertips into the wound. For a fraction of a second he seemed poised to pull the bullet out, but the pain proved too strong and he merely slumped back down.

"It doesn't have to be like this," John stammered, trying to sit up. "We can work together!"

Ignoring him, Michael tried frantically to dig the bullet out, clawing desperately at the side of his own neck and ripping away chunks of flesh; more and more blood was gushing from the wound, but the bullet had already begun to sink deeper into his body and after a few seconds he began to slowly get to his feet. Almost falling back down, he stood for a moment before looking up at the night sky and letting out an agonized scream. His eyes briefly began to change, filling with a yellowish tint before returning to their bloodied state.

"I won't do it!" he snarled. "I refuse! I won't let that *thing* out again!"

"What are you talking about?" John asked.

"I won't be like that!" Michael hissed, turning to him as his eyes changed once more. For a few seconds the humanity seemed to leave his face, replaced by something primal and furious that finally faded away. "It wouldn't help, anyway. I can already feel the silver ripping through my body. I can feel it burning its way to my heart."

"What happened to Lisa?" John asked again.

"Lisa..."

Michael hesitated, before furrowing his brow.

"Lisa will be alright," he said finally, as if he could barely believe what he was saying. "I don't know how, but Lisa... and Eloise... I have to make sure that they're safe. I can't go yet. I can't leave them like this."

"Let me help," John replied, hauling himself up and taking a tentative, stumbling step forward. "There's still time."

"I don't know if I have the strength to get back," Michael stammered as tears filled his eyes, "or the time, but I have to try."

"Tell me what we need to do," John said firmly.

"You?" Michael hesitated for a moment longer, before turning to him. "All you need to do is die."

Before John could reply, Michael lunged at him, slamming him against the tree and knocking him out cold.

CHAPTER SEVENTEEN

Twenty years earlier...

"NO!"

On the ground with her eyes squeezed tight shut, Lisa waited for the end, for the wolf's huge teeth to rip through her body. She could hear a cacophony of howls and snarls and screams ringing in her ears, filling her senses, and a moment later she felt hot blood starting to splatter down onto the side of her face; some of the blood ran down into her mouth as she tried to turn and crawl away, but finally the sounds faded away and she was left in silence. The only thing she could hear now was her own heart pounding in her chest, and another heart pounding somewhere nearby.

And then, slowly, she realized that the

heavier heartbeat nearby was starting to falter, almost as if it might be about to stop altogether.

As soon as she opened her eyes, she saw Michael on his knees nearby. He was holding a knife, and she saw the shock in his eyes as thick blood dripped from the edge of the blade.

Hearing a loud snort, Lisa looked up and saw the large wolf leaning down toward her. Whereas a moment ago the beast had been filled with an almost unbearable fury, now she saw something else entirely; she looked up into one of its eyes and saw a kind of pain that she recognized from her years working as a veterinarian, and she realized in a heartbeat that she was looking at a dying animal. A moment later she realized that blood was running freely from a huge gash that had been cut across the creature's throat, and seconds after that the wolf let out a heavy sigh as it slumped down a little more.

Realizing that she was about to get crushed, Lisa crawled out of the way just in time and watched as the wolf crashed against the ground. Its eye remained focused on her for a few seconds, until she saw the very moment when the life faded away to nothing.

"He's dead," she whispered, before looking back at Michael and once again seeing the bloodied knife in his hand. "Michael, did you..."

Her voice trailed off as she realized that at

the very last second Michael must have intervened and killed his own father. That thought was so impossible to grasp, and she found herself trying to come up with any other explanation, yet deep down she knew exactly what she'd just witnessed.

"Michael," she continued, "what -"

"Move!" he gasped.

"Michael -"

"Move!" he shouted, stumbling to his feet and racing over to her, grabbing her by the hand and hauling her up. "We don't have much time!"

"Michael, what did you do?" she asked.

"Shut up and move!" he hissed, pulling her toward the cabin as the other wolves began to howl into the night air. "Get inside!"

"Michael, stop!" she snapped, almost tripping as he dragged her up the steps that led to the cabin's front door. "Michael, you're hurting me!"

***

As soon as he'd slammed the door shut with his back, Michael dropped the bloodied knife onto the floor. He turned and fumbled with the lock for a moment, before hurrying to the window and looking out as the wolves continued to howl.

"Michael," Lisa said cautiously, her voice trembling with fear, "was that really your..."

She hesitated, before reaching down and

picking up the knife. Holding it out, she saw that the blood was caked all along the blade's edge, with some having run down onto the handle and onto her own hand.

"Was that really your father?" she continued. "Michael, did you just kill your own father?"

"I warned you!" he stammered, still looking out at the wolves that were howling as they stood in a semi-circle around the larger, dead wolf in the center of the clearing. "I warned all of you! I know something bad was going to happen if you didn't back off! Why couldn't everyone leave me alone?"

"You didn't have to do that," she replied, still struggling to accept everything that had happened. Looking down, she saw that the front of her shirt was covered in the large wolf's blood. "There was another way."

"What are you talking about?" he snapped.

"There has to have been another way," she continued. "Michael, I'm so sorry, I thought I was getting through to him. I had no idea that he was going to attack me."

"I warned you."

"Yes, but -"

"I warned you!" he screamed, turning to her with pure anger in his eyes. "How can you say that you didn't know when I warned you? How can you stand there and act like I didn't try to stop you?"

"I know," she replied, holding her hands up, dropping the knife in the process, "but I *was* getting through to him. I was making him understand." She hesitated, before hurrying to the window and looking out at the clearing. "You don't know that he's dead, though," she added, frantically trying to think of some way to make things better. "He's a werewolf, right? Like you? Can't he just change himself and... heal, somehow?"

She waited for an answer, but the wolves outside were howling louder than ever.

"He can do that, right?" she said. "Michael, you've done it before so why can't he?"

"He could recover from pretty much any wound," Michael replied, "except one." He paused for a moment. "It's always been known that the king can only be felled by a wound cut by his own blood."

She turned to him.

"He could only be killed by one of his own sons," he added.

"That doesn't make sense," she replied, before stepping over to the door and reaching for the lock. "I'm a veterinarian, Michael, I might be able to save him. I know it looks bad, but -"

Before she could touch the key, Michael's hand grabbed her arm and held her back.

"Let me try!" she hissed.

"No."

"There's still a chance!" she continued, trying to twist free from his grip. "You have to let me go out there!"

He shook his head.

"Michael -"

"What's done is done," he said, interrupting her, "and there's no going back. I don't know what the consequences will be, but things are about to change. There were rumors that he foresaw his own death coming soon, but I'm sure even he couldn't possibly have imagined that it would be like this. Then again, you never know. For all our disagreements and problems, I never doubted his wisdom."

"I can still help," she replied as tears ran down her cheeks. "Michael, why won't you let me try?"

"Maybe he was right all along," he continued, as if he hadn't even heard her plea. "He always insisted that the two worlds could never mix. He always worried that by coming out here to the cabin and separating myself off from the pack, I was risking the worlds coming together. Perhaps he foresaw all of this, as well. What if I made a terrible mistake? What if I put my own happiness above the needs of the pack?" He paused for a moment longer, still holding Lisa's wrist firmly. "There's only one way to put it right," he added with a growing sense of determination in his voice. "I have to make a stand and prove that all of this can still be saved. It won't be easy, it's going to require a hell of a lot of sacrifice, but we really don't have a choice. I just need to think."

"Michael -"

"I can't do that if you keep talking!" he snapped angrily, before pushing her away from the door. "Be quiet!"

"Fine, but let me go out there," she said, stepping toward the door again. "I might -"

"No!"

Suddenly exploding with rage, he grabbed her by the shoulders and lifted her up, before throwing her across the cabin with such force that she slammed hard against the opposite wall. As she fell down against the wooden boards, she let out a groan of pain, and then she began to sit up before she saw Michael watching her from his position in front of the door. Horrified by his sudden outburst, Lisa waited for him to rush over, or for him to apologize, but instead he simply continued to stare at her for a moment.

"How many times do I have to tell you?" he asked, with pure rage filling his voice. "You don't understand any of this and you've already caused enough trouble. All you can do now, Lisa, is keep your mouth shut and let me figure this all out. And until I've got that done, I need you to stay down there and leave me alone!"

CHAPTER EIGHTEEN

Today...

"I'M SORRY TO HAVE to keep calling," Garrett said, unable to hide the agitation in his voice as he stood in the office at the end of the hospital ward, "but we really need your opinion on this matter, Doctor Law. Can you *please* call me back as soon as you get this message?"

He hesitated, wondering whether there was anything else he could add to emphasize the severity of the situation, before sighing as he cut the call.

"Well?"

Turning, he saw Jessie standing in the doorway.

"He's calm," she continued, sounding utterly

exhausted as she stepped into the room, "at least for now. I don't know what's causing these fits of agitation, though." She wiped sweat from her brow. "I've never known a patient like him. It's as if something else has taken control of his body and it's just... shaking him apart." She paused. "Not that I'm suggesting that's actually what has been happening, of course. I'm just reaching for some kind of explanation."

"I've left three messages for Doctor Law now," Garrett explained, "but he isn't getting back to me. Everyone else is either impossible to get hold of, or busy, or both. Sometimes I feel like something's deliberately stopping us calling for help."

"Something?" she replied. "Like what?"

"I don't know," he continued, slipping past her and heading out into the corridor, "but if the pattern holds, Tommy Wallace should start having another of those fits in the next few minutes. We need to get back there and make sure we're able to hold him down."

"Are you sure that's the best approach?"

Stopping, he turned to her.

"There's no indication of brain activity," she continued. "It's like his mind has gone but his body refuses to die, but he can't carry on like this. I don't know, I just feel as if we're torturing the poor guy by keeping him alive. If there's even the tiniest part of his mind left in there, he must be going through absolute agony."

"I know you're not suggesting that it sounds like you're suggesting," Garrett said firmly.

She opened her mouth to reply, before shaking her head.

"Good," he added. "If you're too tired, take a break. I can handle him for a little while, and eventually we have to find *someone* who'll come and help us out. If not Doctor Law, then someone else. Do you mind trying to put a call through while I go and check on the patient? I'm having no luck at all, and I can't help wondering whether I'm losing my mind."

As Garrett walked away, Jessie picked up the phone and pressed for an outside line, only to find that the usual dial-tone was missing. Instead she heard a faint crackling sound coming from the receiver; she held it closer to her ear, and after a few seconds she began to wonder whether she might be able to hear some kind of whispering voice emerging from the static. This voice was just too buried to be properly audible, but she felt sure that someone on the other end of the line was trying to say something.

"Hello?" she said cautiously. "Is someone there?"

She waited, but the voice merely twisted and shifted in the noise.

"Hello?" she continued. "What are you trying to say? Do you need help?"

She glanced at the phone again, worried that she'd accidentally patched herself through to one of the other wards and that perhaps someone else in the hospital needed help. Once she was sure that she'd pressed the button for an outside line, she took a moment to listen again as the voice persisted.

"Hello?" she said yet again. "Can you tell me what -"

"He's gone!"

Startled, she turned to see that Garrett had rushed back to the doorway.

"Tommy Wallace," he continued, clearly in a state of shock. "What did you do to him, Jessie? I just went to his room and he's not there! Where the hell did he go?"

***

Sitting all alone at the bus stop, Elizabeth Ward stared straight ahead across the dark road and wondered why the bus back into town could *never* be early.

Late, sure, it was late more often than not.

But never early.

As a cold wind blew along the road, whistling through the gasp in the shelter, she looked up and then turned to her left. She could see the lights of the rebuilt Middleford Cross in the distance, and she had to admit that the sight of that place sent a shiver through her bones. She was a Sobolton girl born and bred, she'd never even left the town once, and she knew all the garbled and somewhat mangled stories that people whispered about the hospital. Something had happened there about a decade earlier, something that even the local gossip-mongers had never quite managed to get straight, but ever since the entire area around the building – or the Overflow, as it was known locally – had just seemed to be charged with some extra frisson of disrupted energy.

Almost as if -

Suddenly hearing a rustling sound, Elizabeth turned and looked at the bushes. To her surprise, she saw a thin and rather ill-looking man stepping out from the undergrowth, wearing a hospital gown and trailing various wires and tubes that had clearly once been connected to machines. The man walked barefoot around from behind the shelter, before stopping at the edge of the road with his mouth hanging wide open. Finally, slowly, he turned to look at Elizabeth, and she saw that both his eyes were missing.

She opened her mouth, but in truth she had no idea what to say. She wasn't even sure that such a horrifying vision could be real.

"Have you seen her?" Tommy asked finally,

his voice sounding scratched and fragile.

"Who?" Elizabeth replied, before she had a chance to wonder whether she should engage with the man at all.

"She's awake," Tommy continued, "and I would like to see her one last time, before I go to Sangreth. If this body will permit me to make the journey, at least."

"I'm sure I don't know what you mean," Elizabeth said, pulling her handbag a little closer.

"She must sense me," he replied, looking briefly toward the hospital and then turning the other way, watching the road that snaked its way around the forest and into the center of town. "She will come to me, as I go to her."

He set off again, walking straight past Elizabeth with tottering steps that seemed ready to fail at any time.

"Where are you going?" she asked.

"This way."

"I wouldn't walk into town like that," she told him as he continued to head away from the shelter. "Are you from the hospital? Do they know you're out here all on your own? This isn't the best neighborhood, there are some dodgy folks around, you want to be careful." She waited, but he was still walking away, still trailing the wires and tubes. "Sir, do you need help? Do you need to go back to the hospital? Or there's a bus due soon, it goes right into town and stops near the diner if that's any help, I think..."

Her voice trailed off as she realized that she was being completely ignored.

"Sir?"

She waited, but already she could tell that he was almost too far away to hear her properly, and she really didn't want to raise her voice. Part of her worried that she should go after him, but something about the man had set the hairs standing up on the back of her neck. She turned and looked straight ahead again, and after just a few seconds she realized that she had no idea why she felt so flustered. She blinked a few times, then she looked toward the hospital and saw its lights in the distance; she looked the other way and briefly though that she could see a figure walking away toward the town, although after a few seconds she supposed that this must just be a trick of the shadows.

Flinching, she felt a brief flicker of pain in the back of her head, but mercifully this passed quickly and she raised both eyebrows as she checked her watch and saw the time. Usually the minutes ticked by so slowly when she was waiting for the bus home after her late shift at the residential home, but now time seemed to have hopped ahead by a good few minutes while she'd been thinking about... something else. She couldn't quite remember the details.

Now, sitting all alone at the bus stop, Elizabeth Ward stared straight ahead across the dark road and wondered why the bus back into town could *never* be early.

Late, sure, it was late more often than not.

But never early.

CHAPTER NINETEEN

Twenty years earlier...

"GODDAMN FOREST," JOE HICKS muttered as he stumbled through the darkness, bumping into several trees as he tried to keep the flashlight's beam aiming forward. "Sometimes I think someone oughta just pave over the whole damn place with concrete. That'd sort out the problems once and for all, and then we wouldn't need -"

Suddenly hearing a rustling sound, he turned and shone his flashlight back the way he'd just come. Having made the decision to venture out after Lisa alone, he knew there was no way he should have caught up to her just yet.

"Anyone there?" he called out. "If it's one of you boys, you need to know that your daddy specifically called me to come out here tonight, and I went through that fancy gate the right way, just to show that I'm being respectful."

He waited, but already he was starting to believe that he'd perhaps just been a little jumpy.

"Check with him if you need to," he added, just to be extra safe. "That's fine by me. Better to check, than to blunder into some kind of... diplomatic incident."

Again he waited, and then – satisfied that he was alone after all – he turned to continue on his way.

"What the -"

Startled by the sight of someone standing directly ahead, he pulled back and bumped against a tree, dropping his flashlight in the process. He reached down and picked it up, and when he shone the beam ahead he saw a woman smiling at him from just a few feet away.

"What are you doing out here?" he stammered, looking her up and down for a moment. "Who the hell are you?"

"You're lost," she replied.

"I'm no such thing," he insisted, adjusting the collar of his shirt. "I happen to know this area better than I know the back of my hand. I know exactly where I am. I asked you a question, so how about you answer it?"

"I didn't say that you don't know where you

are," she said calmly. "I said that you're lost."

"Then -"

Joe hesitated for a moment, before shaking his head.

"Lady," he continued, "I don't know who you are or what you're doing out here, but you certainly don't look like you're dressed for the outdoors. You're gonna catch pneumonia if you go wandering around like this, so how about you get home and I'll be on my way, okay? Ordinarily I'd haul your skinny ass back to the station and make you tell me what you're up to, but you're lucky that I'm busy tonight on official business. So just go home and get some sleep."

"You're lost," she said again.

"And you're clearly stuck on repeat," he muttered. "Or are you on drugs? Is that what this is about? Listen, I don't have time for this nonsense, alright? I happen to be out here on very serious and very important police business, and right now you're distracting me from that business. I'm not lost, I don't need help and I know exactly where I'm going. Which is more than can be said for you, as it happens. Do you even have a gun with you?"

"Why would I need a gun?" she asked. "Am I in danger?"

"Well -"

"There aren't any wolves around here, are there?"

"Well, no," he said cautiously, furrowing his brow, "as it happens, there aren't any wolves at all. But that still doesn't mean that you can go wandering around like this. Where do you live, anyway?"

"I have a little place up past Cutter's Hill," she told him.

"Then I'd strongly suggest that you go there," he said, stepping past her and pushing on through the forest. "I don't mean to be rude, but I really don't have time to stop and chat. I should warn you, though, that if I bump into you again on my way back I'll have no choice, I'll have to arrest you and take you to the station for questioning. I'm sure you don't want that to happen, so please just get lost, alright?"

He was still muttering away to himself and complaining out loud as he disappeared into the darkness, leaving the ghost of Amanda Mathis standing alone as she listened to the sound of him getting further and further away.

"You're lost," she whispered calmly, "but that's fine. One day, many years from now, the wolves will find you. And when that day comes, they will tear you limb from limb."

***

"Goddammit!" Joe spluttered a short while later,

smashing his way through another overgrown section of the forest, before finally stopping and slamming an enraged fist against one of the trees. "I'm too old for this shit! And I'm not even old! I'm just -"

Before he could finish, he realized that he could hear a strange howling sound coming from nearby. He froze, immediately aware that this could signal trouble, and slowly he turned and looked to his left as he realized that the howling sound seemed to be coming from several wolves all at once. He'd heard similar sounds plenty of times in the past, of course, but something was different now; the more he listened, the more Joe began to realize that this particular sound was filled with some other quality. Something almost like...

Sorrow.

Swallowing hard, he picked his way through the undergrowth. Whereas before he'd been blundering along with scant care for delicacy, now he was trying to be as quite as possible. He even lowered his flashlight, until finally he reached the edge of the clearing and saw that he'd arrived at his destination. Already he could see the cabin on the clearing's other side, but right now he was more focused on the chorus of wolves that had gathered all around the open space. Stopping, he saw a large shape on the ground, and somehow deep down he already understood that this was a place of death.

He opened his mouth to call out, but at the last second even Joe realized that he should keep his mouth shut. He couldn't help stepping forward, however, and squinting a little in an attempt to see better in the moonlight.

"It's you," he said silently, moving his lips but refraining from making any actual sound.

Suddenly one of the wolves turned and looked straight at him. Joe froze again; he'd seen this particular wolf many times before, and he knew its one-eyed glare well enough. He instinctively reached for his gun, even though he knew he could never fight off an entire pack. The other wolves quickly turned to him as well, and in his panicked state Joe had already clocked that there must be more than a dozen of the damn things. He put his hand on his gun and waited, and now his heart was racing as he tried to wonder how he was going to defend himself. In his mind's eye, he saw himself getting torn to shreds, and he imagined his own bloodied remains bleeding into the mud.

And then, with no warning, the wolves fell silent and ran, each turning and racing off into the forest until – in a matter of seconds – they'd disappeared entirely from view.

"What the..."

This time Joe actually said the words out loud. He waited a moment longer, still poised to draw his gun, and then he stepped forward again and made his way into the clearing. Still looking all around, still convinced that more wolves were about to appear at any moment, he nevertheless approached the large dead creature in the middle of the clearing, stepping cautiously around the hulking corpse until he saw its eyes. Death stared back up at him, and in the moonlight Joe could see that the beast's throat had been ripped open. For a moment, the sight was one of awe-inspiring contemplation – at least, it would have been for anyone else.

"Not so smug now, are you?" Joe sneered, kicking the side of the wolf's jaw. "Got any lectures for me? Any mysterious pronouncements that you can't quite be bothered to explain?"

He waited again.

"No?"

He paused, and then he kicked the wolf harder.

"I didn't think so," he muttered, before allowing himself a faint chuckle. "I always knew this day'd come." He let out a derisory snort. "Yeah, I always knew. You always went prancing around, acting like you were the boss of everywhere, but I knew deep down that one day you'd end up like this. Too bad you're not as smart as you thought you were."

He paused again, before kicking the wolf's open dead eye.

"If there's one trait I truly deplore," he

continued, "it's arrogance. Arrogance and -"

Suddenly he heard a brief, terrified cry ringing out from the cabin. A woman's cry. Startled, Joe drew his gun and turned, aiming directly at the cabin's door. Already the cry had faded away, leaving the clearing to silence once more, but Joe's heart was pounding and deep down he knew that he recognized that cry.

"Lisa Sondnes," he whispered through gritted teeth. "Why couldn't you leave well enough alone?"

CHAPTER TWENTY

Today...

SLOWLY, AND WITH A sudden sense of pain, John Tench began to open his eyes. For a few seconds he had no idea what had happened, no clue at all, but he quickly realized that he was on the ground in the forest. He blinked, and suddenly everything came rushing back.

"I don't know if I have the strength to get back," he remembered the strange, bloodied man muttering, "or the time, but I have to try."

"Tell me what we need to do," John had replied.

"You?" the man had hesitated for a moment longer, before turning to him. "All you need to do is die."

Then he'd attacked, launching himself at John. Now, as his mind began to clear and as he started to haul himself to his feet, John remembered the fraction of a second after the man had slammed into his chest. He remembered falling back and hitting his head, probably on one of the trees, and he realized that in that flash of time he'd truly believed that the end was near, that he was going to die; and as those thoughts had filled his head, he'd been horrified by one terrible realization. His life hadn't flashed before his eyes, there'd been nothing as simple as that; instead, in the split second before passing out, he'd thought of the one person who still mattered.

His son.

Shaking his head, he reached back and felt a sore spot just above his neck. At the same time, his broken fingers were starting to burn with pain. Telling himself that this was no time to be maudlin, and that he'd done as much as he could with Nick anyway, he looked around and saw that there was no sign of the bloodied man now. Puzzled, and still convinced that the man had been planning to kill, John stepped over to his flashlight and picked it up; pushing through the pain in his fingers, he switched the flashlight back on and turned, aiming the beam between the trees. He half expected to see the bloodied figure nearby, to find that he was merely being toyed with in his final moments, but instead he froze as he finally spotted the one-eyed wolf staring back at him nearby.

"Hey," John stammered, holding up one hand, fully aware that he had no chance of defending himself. "I'm not -"

Before he could finish, the wolf turned and ran, racing away into the distance. John heard the furious rush of the creature bounding though the undergrowth, until that soon too faded to nothing.

"Well," John continued, raising both eyebrows as he realized that he wasn't having much luck anticipating matters, "that seems like -"

Suddenly a wolf howled in the distance, followed a moment later by another howl that seemed to emerge from another part of the forest as a kind of response. For a few seconds, John couldn't help but feel that he was listening to some kind of message getting passed along. Before he had a chance to consider what that might mean, however, he spotted something dark and wet glistening on the trunk of a nearby tree. He made his way over and raised the flashlight, and when he peered at the substance he was already able to tell what he'd found.

"Blood," he whispered, as he looked a little further and saw a second bloodied hand-print on another tree. "You're injured. You didn't have the strength to finish me off, so you ran instead."

He hesitated, but he already knew that he

had to try to follow the hand-prints. After all, the bloodied man was clearly responsible for what had happened to Tommy Wallace, and John had no intention of letting him get away. Although he still wasn't quite sure how to bring the bastard to justice, he told himself – as he set off following the trail of blood – that he'd figure something out when the moment arrived.

***

Another wolf howled in the distance, far off in the forest, but John had begun to ignore that sound now. As he picked his way between more trees, navigating a patch of sloping ground, he knew that something was going on all around but he told himself that he had to focus on the task at hand. And as he steadied himself against another tree, he realized that above the sound of howling wolves he could actually hear something more immediately important.

Running water.

He pushed through the forest for a few more minutes, occasionally spotting a tell-tale patch of blood that suggested he was on the right track, before reaching the edge of a small rocky outcrop and spotting a figure standing ahead, silhouetted against the full moon in the night sky. Instinctively reaching for his gun, and finding it missing, John already knew that he'd tracked down his man.

And this time, he wasn't going to let him get away.

"Enough now!" he called out, stepping beyond the trees and onto the outcrop, which he realized now was rising up over the spot where two rivers met far below. He wasn't entirely sure of his location, but he figured that he must be somewhere out past Henge Cliff. "You're injured. You have to come with me now."

"I don't *have* to do anything," Michael replied wearily, staring down at the rivers and listening for a moment to the sound of water crashing together. "You don't have more of those silver bullets, and even if you did, you've lost the element of surprise. I've got to admit that you surprised me, though, more than any simple man has ever done before. I think I might have underestimated you."

"You're under arrest," John said firmly.

"Michael."

"I'm sorry?"

"You asked me my name," Michael continued, clearly struggling now to get any words out at all. After a moment he turned and glared at him, and the pain was visible all across his face. "I don't think I told you. Or perhaps I did and I forgot. Anyway, my name is Michael."

"Do you have a surname, Michael?"

"Don't be greedy. You've already got more than most men."

"Michael," John said after a moment, struggling to keep hold of the flashlight with his broken, crippled fingers. "I admit that I don't understand exactly what's going on out here tonight, but you committed a very serious attack tonight on one of my men. He's in a hospital bed right now, fighting for his life, and if you think I'm going to let you go then... I'm sorry, Michael, but it's not going to work like that."

"All I ever wanted was for her to be happy," Michael replied through gritted teeth. "Why wasn't that enough? I wanted her to be happy, and safe and... mine, forever. And that's what she wanted, she told me at the beginning that she loved me, she fought back and remembered our love even when everyone else tried to make her forget forever. She proved to me that her love was genuine, even though she didn't need to prove anything at all. So why wasn't she happy when I gave her everything she'd ever asked for?"

"I don't know what you're talking about," John said, before pausing for a moment. "Michael... are you talking about Lisa Sondnes?"

"It's not my fault!" Michael snapped angrily. "I did everything, and I still ended up like this." He paused again, before holding up his trembling hands. "The silver works its way through our bodies," he explained. "It binds to our increased iron levels, at least that's what I was told once. It binds and then it infects, and it hurts so much as it rots us from the inside, eating through our blood and leaving our bodies as nothing more than husks. There's rarely anything that can be done, and even if there was, I refuse to suffer the indignity of clinging pathetically to this life. That's one lesson, at least, that my father taught me well."

"Michael," John replied, "I need you to step away from the edge."

"I suffered for her," Michael sneered. "After she saw my other form, I swore I'd never change again. I swore that I'd remain human forever, just for her. And I kept that promise, I've been in my human form for forty years, even though the pain has been immeasurable. Why didn't she understand that I was proving my love all along? Why didn't she see that I was only ever trying to make her safe?"

"Michael -"

"I'm a king!" he screamed suddenly, shaking with rage. "I'm the king of this forest and all I wanted was a little respect! Is that too much to ask? Don't look at me like I'm some kind of primitive, common beast! I'm not like my father, I didn't demand to be adored and feared, but I at least wanted to be treated with a little respect!" He held up his hands again; already the flesh around the bullet wound was turning black, almost fizzing as it burned. "I didn't want to be the king, but after I killed him I had no choice! All I wanted was for Lisa to stay by my side and support me! She was going to be my queen, and instead..."

His voice trailed off.

"Instead *what*?" John asked cautiously. He waited for an answer, before taking a solitary step forward. "Michael -"

"I hope she burns in Hell for what she did to me," Michael said darkly. "I hope she spends eternity regretting the way she treated me. I hope it hurts."

"Michael -"

"And I hope this whole kingdom suffers," he added, turning to John once more. "All of it. The forest. The town. The ecotone. Every scrap of land. I hope it all goes to Hell. Because I'm done with it now. I'm done with the whole ungrateful so-called kingdom I inherited. I couldn't care less what happens to any of it, except that I hope one day they'll all realize how badly they treated me. I hope *she* realizes. But for now..."

He paused for a moment, before taking a step back, then another.

"I abdicate."

"Michael!"

In that instant, Michael took yet another step back, and this time he toppled over the edge. For a fraction of a second, as he instinctively reached out, John saw a flash of fear in the other man's bloodied eyes.

And then he was gone.

"Michael!" John shouted again, rushing to the edge and stopping to look over, just in time to see Michael's body slam into a rock and then roll into the river, quickly disappearing beneath the surface.

He waited, but over the next few minutes John saw no sign of Michael at all. The rivers ran fast after meeting, and John realized that the body would most likely have been swept away already. For a moment he wondered whether there was a chance Michael might have survived, but he knew that in his final moments Michael had seemed to have completely given up, as if he had certainly expected to meet his end.

As he continued to look down at the river, John heard a wolf howling nearby, then another, then a couple more. Soon the entire forest seemed to be filled with the sound of a wolf chorus, as if the entire forest was filling with the news of Michael's death.

CHAPTER TWENTY-ONE

Twenty years earlier...

"LISA!" JOE SHOUTED AS he made his way past the dead wolf and headed toward the steps that led up to the cabin. "Lisa Sondnes, it's me! It's Joe Hicks, I just want to talk and -"

Before he could finish, the cabin's door swung open and Michael stepped out into the moonlight.

"Well," Joe said, stopping and staring up at him for a moment, before tilting his head slightly, "you look about as bad as a man can look without being six feet under."

"You have no business here," Michael said firmly.

"And on that we're in agreement," Joe

replied, already trying to look past him and see inside the cabin. "The thing is, I reckon Lisa doesn't have any business here either. So why don't I just take her off your hands and lead her back to town? That way, we can make sure that everyone's where they ought to be rather than having all this... mixing."

"My father is dead," Michael told him.

"Yeah, I kinda figured that," Joe said, turning and looking at the corpse. "Tell me, though, is this real death or do you wolfy types have a way of cheating that?"

"There are only two things that can kill us," Michael replied. "Silver, as you well know, kills most of us. My father managed to make himself immune to that as king, but the rest of us... And the other thing that does the job is if we're murdered by our own bloodline. Children, specifically. By the end of his life, pretty much the only thing that could possibly have killed my father was one of his own sons."

"Oh?"

Joe turned to him and stared for a moment.

"Oh," he added.

"Yeah," Michael replied, "so as you can imagine, this all only happened within the last few hours, so we're kind of adjusting to a new reality."

"So the king's dead," Joe said carefully, watching Michael closely, "so... long live the new king, right? Whoever he might be." He waited for an answer. "Who *is* the new king?"

"I suppose you're looking at him," Michael replied.

"Huh," Joe muttered, before pausing for a moment, lost in thought. "Huh," he manage again.

"I didn't ask for any of this," Michael continued. "I just wanted to hide away from it all, but I should have realized that I didn't have a chance. So here I am, king against my will, and now I guess I have to rule. Things are going to be a little different around here from now on, Sheriff Hicks. Don't worry, I'm very much going to leave the town of Sobolton alone, provided the people of that town return the favor. I have no desire to interfere. I know how disastrous it would be if our two worlds mixed."

"That's pretty much how I've always read it," Joe admitted.

"My people have tolerated your intrusions," Michael added. "Your little incursions into our forest. When you cut down those trees and built those pylons and ran your electricity supply through our forest, we considered that to be an act of war, but we showed remarkable restraint. We've barely touched the supply since, apart from one or two periodic reminders of our frustration."

"It's just a few pylons and cable," Joe pointed out.

"They burn our minds!" Michael snapped angrily. "You might not feel it in your own petty little heads, but we're far more sensitive to these things. But we accepted it anyway, more or less, and you should be glad of that fact. And I'm going to keep the peace, just as my father did, so long as you make sure that the people of Sobolton don't go around damaging the rest of our home."

"You've got my word on that," Joe told him. "I've always -"

Before he could finish, Joe heard a loud bumping sound coming from inside the cabin.

"Can I see Lisa?" he asked.

"Not right now."

"I just want to see that she's alright."

"Lisa's here with me now," Michael replied. "If it helps, you can think of her as my queen. Against all the advice of all the elders in history, I've chosen to take someone from your world and bring here into my home, and she'll be living here with me now. You don't have to worry, though. She's not your problem, not now, and she won't ever be again. I want her apartment kept exactly as it is now, as a reminder of her absence from your world, but other than that I'd like it if everyone in Sobolton simply forgets about her. She can't straddle two worlds. No-one can. So she's here with me now."

"I'd still like to see her," Joe said cautiously.

"So you can steal her away from me again?"

"I didn't say -"

"I should have torn you limb from limb for that," Michael snarled. "Instead I chose to accept it as a test, as a way for her to prove that nothing could hold our love back. And she passed that test with flying colors, despite your attempts to stop her. That's how pure love works, Sheriff Hicks, although I doubt you'd know much about that." He paused for a moment. "I know my father used to reach out to you occasionally, sometimes he'd enter your mind and talk to you. I want you to understand that I won't be doing that."

"Fine by me," Joe said, "but if we need to communicate, then how do -"

"We won't," Michael said firmly.

"You can't be sure of that."

"I can," Michael continued. "I can be sure of anything I *want* to be sure of, because I have the power to make it so. My father's mind might still be around for a little while, just a decade or two. That's how death works for us. He won't try to speak to me, he'll be too ashamed, but he might speak to you on occasion and try to still influence this world. If he does, I want you to ignore him completely. Pretend he's not around at all, and eventually he'll fade away. It's always sad when an old king lingers, but they all get the message eventually. Now go and -"

The bumping sound returned briefly.

Michael turned and looked back into the cabin, waiting for a few seconds until silence had been restored.

"That all seems good to me," Joe said cautiously, adjusting his collar slightly as it began to feel a little tight, "but I'd still quite like to see Lisa briefly, just to really be sure that she's alright out here and that she's happy with the arrangement. I know this might sound kinda stupid, but her father was a good friend of mine and I'd sure feel better if I could just set eyes on her for a second or two."

He waited, but Michael was still looking back into the cabin.

"Can I do that?" Joe added, before taking a step forward. "Or I can just come inside and -"

"Stay back!" Michael snarled, turning to him.

"No problem!" Joe replied, stopping and immediately holding his hands up in some kind of surrender. "Sorry, I didn't mean to cross a line, I just really want to see Lisa."

"You can't."

"Lisa?" Joe called out, craning his neck in an attempt to see properly into the cabin. "I know you lied to me before, but that's okay. I was trying to keep you away from all of this, but if it's what you really want then -"

"She doesn't care what you have to say," Michael said firmly. "If my father speaks to you again, tell him to stay the hell out of my business, and tell him that I'll slaughter anyone else who tries to get involved. Is that clear?"

"Sounds pretty clear to me," Joe replied.

"Sometimes my father was too lenient with you," Michael continued. "I'm going to give you one warning, and one warning only. From now on, Sheriff Hicks, there will be no communication between our worlds. You already know how things work, so I would strongly suggest that you enforce the rules as they exist now. You should also try to pass on your knowledge to someone who can continue your work once you're gone, because – let's face it – you're not getting any younger. For all your many faults, you seem like a man who understands the way things have to be. I trust that I won't have to make a more forceful effort to impose my will."

"I think we have an understanding," Joe said, before hesitating as if there was still something else he wanted to add. "My work here is done, and I'm just gonna head back to the town and focus on keeping the place safe from now on. What you do out here is your concern. You can say a lot of things about me, but I've never been one for sticking my beak into another man's keyhole. Trust me."

"Leave," Michael said, his voice brimming with barely-restrained anger. "Now."

"Bye, then," Joe replied, before looking past

Michael one last time. "Bye, Lisa. I hope you enjoy your new life out here as... queen."

He waited a moment, just in case he might hear an answer, and then he turned and began to walk away.

"I never like you anyway," he sneered at the dead large wolf as he passed. Reaching the edge of the clearing, he turned to see that Michael had already shut the cabin's door. "God bless you, Lisa," he added darkly, before making the sign of the cross against his chest. "Whatever happens... you can't ever say that I didn't do my best to keep you out of it."

CHAPTER TWENTY-TWO

Today...

LIMPING ALONG ANOTHER DARK street near the edge of town, Doctor Robert Law leaned heavily on his cane. He didn't even know where he was going, not exactly, but he couldn't just go home and pretend nothing bad was happening. Instead, even though his knees were hurting and he was getting short of breath, he pushed on through the night in a desperate attempt to find the little girl.

And then, finally, he turned the next corner and saw her.

But not just her.

"Tommy?" he whispered.

For a moment he could only stare at the bizarre, incongruous sight of the little girl standing in front of Tommy Wallace – who was still wearing his hospital gown – and looking up at the man's eyeless face. Robert squinted slightly, and now he realized that the pair of them were actually engaged in some kind of conversation. Worried that he might have lost his mind, and that he might be imagining things, Robert watched for a few seconds longer before starting to make his way slowly and a little unsteadily along the street, determined to get closer and hear what was being said. At the same time, a cold wind blew through the town, rustling the trees that marked the start of the forest.

Once he'd reached the opposite sidewalk, Robert was finally about to make out the words coming from the girl's lips.

"But why can't you stay?" she was asking. "I don't understand."

"My time is over," Tommy replied, staring down at her despite the thick bandages covering his empty eye sockets. "I have spent twenty years watching over my kingdom since my death, and now is the time for me to depart. You will understand why. Eventually."

"I'm scared," the girl said.

"And you have every reason to be," Tommy said, "but you're old enough now. The time is coming when you must allow yourself to grow up."

"I don't want to."

"Neither did I, once," Tommy replied, "but

then -"

Suddenly he turned and looked straight at Robert. Already, fresh blood was soaking through from his eye sockets, spreading across the bandages. A moment later the little girl turned and looked as well.

"The good doctor is here," Tommy continued, with a faint smile. "He's not a stranger to the forest. He has even been to the gate I built toward the end of my reign, although he had the good sense to show respect."

"He's the man I told you about," the girl replied, furrowing her brow. "After I came out of the ice, when I was still trying to sleep, he cut me open and examined my insides. It took all my strength not to scream."

"He's one of them," Tommy explained. "You mustn't be scared. Not really. They're all really rather harmless. However, they can be useful from time to time. This one, for example, carries terrible guilt. He would be a perfect candidate for the warning we have already discussed."

"I guess so," the girl said softly, with no evident enthusiasm. "If you really think I have to."

"It is your duty," Tommy said, before turning to her again and smiling. "But now I really must go." He reached out and put a hand on her shoulder. "The bloodline is secure, even if I had to wait before I could be sure of that. Recent events will have destabilized matters, and you will have to work hard to put it all right. I am confident, however, that I'm leaving it all in your capable hands."

"I'll do my best," she replied cautiously.

"Tommy," Robert said, holding out a hand as he stepped forward, "what the hell are you doing out here? You're supposed to be at the hospital!"

"You sound so funny," Tommy replied, as the smile on his lips grew wider. "You will not be... not..."

His voice trailed off; although the smile remained on his lips, something about his expression seemed very static now, almost frozen in place as an almost imperceptible sense of horror began to spread slowly across his face. Fresh blood seeped out from beneath one of the bandages, spreading slowly across the fabric directly covering what had once been Tommy's left eye, and finally he reached up with both hands and began to feel the bandages' frayed edges.

"What... what's happened to me?" he gasped, still touching his face as if he couldn't quite believe what he was feeling. "Why am I... what -"

Suddenly he dropped to his knees. He began to pull at the bandages, trying to rip them away while muttering frantically to himself.

"Tommy, stop that!" Robert hissed, hurrying over to him. "For the love of God, what are you doing?"

"Why can't I see?" Tommy shouted, ripping one of the bandages away to reveal the hollow socket, then touching the edges before slipping his fingertips inside. "Where's my eye?" he whimpered. "What have you done to me?" He pulled the other bandage away, exposing the other socket. "Why can't I see?" he screamed. "Help! Somebody help me!"

"We need to get you back to the hospital," Robert replied, putting a hand on Tommy's shoulder. "Listen to me, I'm going to call help, okay? I don't know how you've ended up out here, but we're going to get you back to the hospital and then everything's going to be just fine." He pulled his work phone out; his hands were trembling as he tried to find the number for the ward. "Just give me a moment," he stammered. "This one's trickier than my other phone. Damn it, why can't I just do this?"

After a couple of attempts, he managed to tap the screen in the right spot, dialing the number. He waited, but already he could hear static fizzing from the speakers, although moments later a voice emerged.

"Doctor Law?" Garrett said, his words barely audible at all as the static buzz grew louder. "I've been trying to -"

In that moment, the phone flew from Robert's hands with such force that it spun out across the street and hit one of the trees, instantly shattering and sending the broken pieces falling down onto the ground. Shocked, Robert stared at the phone's remains for a moment before slowly turning to see the little girl glaring at him from just a few feet away.

"Did you do that?" he gasped.

"Why did you cut me open?" she asked.

"I..."

For a few seconds, unable to believe what was happening, Robert could only stare at her. Finally he reached out, daring to touch the side of her face, although he immediately pulled back as he realized that she felt warm. He hesitated, and then he touched her again, this time letting the side of his finger linger against her cheek.

"You're alive," he whispered. "I mean, you have to be, because you're standing right in front of me but... you're really alive, aren't you?"

"Why did you cut me open?" she continued. "Why did you take out my brain and weigh it? Why did you crack my ribs? Why did you take out my heart?"

"I was conducting an autopsy," he replied. "You were... I mean, you *are*..."

Unable to finish that sentence, he instead pressed two fingers against the side of her neck; sure enough, he felt a strong and healthy heartbeat.

"This isn't possible," he added. "Even for a

town like Sobolton, this can't be happening."

"I was so cold and lonely," she told him. "You put me into a dark place, when all I needed was to be warm after the ice. I was cold, and that meant that it took much longer for me to get better. I should make you feel all the horrible things that you did to me. As punishment."

"I'm a doctor," he replied, as tears began to stream down his face. "I was doing my job!"

"Don't worry," she continued. "I'm not going to hurt you. My grandfather wouldn't like that. Besides, I think he wants me to do something else, and that'll probably be enough of a punishment."

"What do you mean?" Robert asked. "I don't know what -"

Before he could finish, she reached out and put a hand on the side of his face.

"I've never done this before," she said softly, "so it might not go as well as it should, but I'll do my best. Mom never likes it when I do anything like this, but I don't have a choice. And it'll only be short, it'll only take a few seconds although... I think it might feel like much longer."

"Who are you?" Robert asked, as he felt the girl's fingertips somehow reaching deep into his mind, stirring his thoughts. "*What* are you?"

"I'm a sign of things to come," she said through gritted teeth. "I'm a sign of a future that we both have to stop."

CHAPTER TWENTY-THREE

Twenty years earlier...

"BOSS? YOU'RE BACK LATE."

Stopping in the doorway, Joe Hicks looked over at the desk and saw Carolyn in her usual seat. He blinked a couple of times before realizing that some paperwork lay spread across the desk, and finally he let out a sigh as he remembered that he'd asked her to go through some of the documents relating to an upcoming court appearance.

"I'm sorry," he said, making his way over and stopping for a moment, "I just... I didn't think you'd be here."

"Are you okay?" she asked. "You look... different."

"I'm going to my office," he replied,

stepping around the corner and starting to make his way along the corridor, while reaching up to once again loosen his collar. "I don't want to be disturbed. If any calls come in, let the boys on the night duty handle it."

Stopping suddenly, he paused for a few seconds before heading back to the desk.

"How?" he added.

"I'm sorry?"

"You said I look different," he continued. "How?"

"Oh, I didn't mean any offense by it," she replied. "I just thought you look a little... pale. And worried, too. It's probably the stress of your recent promotion. I bet you've got people coming at you from all angles, asking you for things and just... bugging you."

"I sure do," he told her.

"You'll get used to it, though," she added, offering a tentative smile. "I know you're gonna smash it."

"I hope so," he replied, before looking at the paperwork again. "Is there anything in there about Lisa Sondnes?"

"The veterinarian?" She furrowed her brow. "No. Should there be?"

"I want you to pull together every case file, and every report, that mentions her name," Joe said. "Even if it's something that seems insignificant, I want you to gather it all up for me. Can you do that?"

"Sure."

"Tonight."

"Tonight?" She paused again. "Joe, is something wrong?" She waited for an answer. "Did something happen? Is Lisa Sondnes okay?"

"Lisa Sondnes is..."

His voice trailed off. A moment later he spun around, convinced that he'd heard the sound of a wolf howling somewhere in the distance, although he quickly reminded himself that he was too far from the forest to ever hear such a thing. The wolves, which everyone insisted weren't even there at all, could never be sensed from the town, and that was exactly how things were supposed to stay. Forever.

"It's a delicate and evolving situation," he said finally, trying to hide the fear in his voice as he turned back to Carolyn. "I'll explain more in the morning. For now, just get those files together and bring them through to me as soon as you're ready. If anyone comes asking about Lisa, anyone at all, tell them you don't know a damn thing. Is that clear?"

"Crystal," she replied.

She waited, but for a moment Joe seemed lost in thought.

"Scratch that," he added after a few more seconds. "When you've got the files, don't bother bringing them to me. I want you to burn them."

"Burn then?"

"Are you deaf?" he asked. "That's what I said, isn't it? Burn them. Anything that mentions Lisa Sondnes at all, I want it burned. Do you understand?"

"Yes," she stammered, clearly shocked by the order.

"Good," he murmured, before turning and shuffling away along the corridor.

Leaning around the corner, Carolyn watched as Joe disappeared into his office, and a moment later the door swung shut. Puzzled, Carolyn looked back down at the papers on her desk; she was almost done preparing everything for the court, but something in Joe's voice told her that she really needed to get on with the task of finding paperwork related to Lisa Sondnes. Getting to her feet, she headed over to the filing cabinet and began to search, although a moment later the lights briefly flickered off before buzzing back to life.

"Not now," she said firmly, glancing up at the light above her head before looking down one more into the filing cabinet's drawer. "The last thing I need at the moment is another blackout."

***

Whiskey poured out from the bottle, filling the glass

until the halfway point before Joe set the bottle back down. He picked up the glass and swirled the whiskey around for a moment, and then he downed every last drop in one go.

Letting out a gasp, he set the glass on the table again. He hesitated, and then he began to pour himself some more.

"I'm worried about Lisa," he heard Rod's voice saying, emerging from the shadows in the corner of the office, echoing through from twenty years earlier. "Joe, I think something's really wrong with her. I think she's getting... tangled up in things that she ought to leave well alone. Do you understand what I mean?"

"All too well," Joe whispered now, and he figured those were more or less the exact same words he'd used all those years ago.

"I don't know what to do," Rod continued. "I mean, I think I know what I *should* do, but she's my daughter. I want to help her, but I also can't hurt her."

"There's a place for that," Joe said now, and once more his words echoed the past. "It's called Lakehurst. They'll set her straight."

"And can they make her... forget things?"

"Oh, they can do that," Joe said, as he felt a ripple of dread running through his chest. "They can do -"

Suddenly a hand touched his shoulder from

behind. Startled, he spun around and let go of the whiskey glass, letting it fall and shatter on the floor. Looking across the office, Joe saw that there was nobody else around; he knew that he was alone, yet the hand on his shoulder had felt so very real and he certainly wasn't a man given to imagining things. Reaching up, he wiped sweat from his brow before crouching down and starting to gather up the pieces of broken glass.

Above him, the lights flickered again.

"Damn it," he muttered, as more sweat ran down his face. He picked up one of the larger pieces of broken glass, turning it around in the process. "I'm not even -"

And then he saw it.

As the lights flickered again, Joe realized that this particular broken glass shard was showing him a reflection that couldn't possibly be real. He squinted and leaned closer, and he saw what appeared to be his own body slumped on the forest floor, with a wolf leaning close and starting to rip him apart; a second wolf quickly appeared, and a shiver ran through Joe's chest as he realized that he was watching himself getting torn to pieces. No matter how much he wanted to look away, he couldn't help but watch as the horrific scene unfolded, until finally he realized that there was another face in the reflection, that a man was standing further back and watching everything that happened. The man appeared to be wearing a uniform, and he was standing on the other side of the makeshift gate that the wolves had constructed using three of the bodies from the bus crash. Squinting harder, Joe tried to make out the man's features but -

In that moment the door opened. Shocked, Joe turned and saw Carolyn carrying some papers into the room, but in that instant he inadvertently squeezed his hand tight on the broken glass. Letting out a gasp of pain, he looked back down; the strange reflection was gone, but blood was flowing from a cut in his palm.

"Damn it!" he hissed, getting to his feet as he held up the glass shard and turned it around, checking that the strange reflection was really gone.

"Boss?" Carolyn said, setting the papers down and hurrying around to him. "What happened? Did you hurt yourself?"

"I'm fine," he muttered, wiping his hand on the side of his uniform, then grabbing some tissues from a box on the desk.

"You're bleeding! I'll fetch the -"

"I said I'm fine!" he hissed, turning to her and struggling to resist the temptation to strike her on the side of her goddamn face. "Woman, will you just leave me alone?"

"I'm sorry," she replied, clearly shocked by the anger in his voice She took a step back, and then she made her way over to the door. "I think there are a few more files with Lisa's name in them. I'll go to the storeroom now. You should get that hand looked at, though. There's a kit in the break room with bandages and stuff. Let me know if you need any help."

"I don't need help from anyone!" he snarled, waiting until she was gone before picking up the piece of broken glass again. He turned it around, but now he saw nothing out of the ordinary, just a glimpse of his own reflection. "I'm just getting spooked and letting my imagination run wild, that's all. I'm damn near losing my mind just because of some stupid trick of the light."

As he took some more tissues and began to wipe blood from the cut on his hand, he paid little attention to the light that was still occasionally flickering and buzzing above.

CHAPTER TWENTY-FOUR

Today...

THE WOLF LEANED IN closer, grabbing hold of a patch of fabric and starting to pull; the fabric refused to break free, however, so the wolf began to pull harder and harder, letting out a faint growl as it jerked the corner with all its strength. Finally the entire dumpster began to topple over, and the wolf pulled back as bags of garbage crashed down and dirty water spread out across the cracked concrete.

"What's that thing doing here?" Robert Law asked, leaning on his stick as he limped around behind the diner and watched the wolf hurrying away. The animal briefly turned and looked at him before scurrying around the corner. "They're not usually brave enough to come into the town."

"Sometimes things change," the little girl said, following him just a few paces behind.

Robert turned to her. Before he had a chance to ask another question, however, he spotted another wolf in the distance. This particular wolf looked much weaker than any he'd ever seen before, almost emaciated, and Robert couldn't help but feel sorry for the poor creature as it limped slowly across the far end of the parking lot. In that moment, however, he realized that something about the entire town seemed different, and as he turned and looked the other way he noticed that there were no lights in any of the buildings. In fact, apart from the wolves that now roamed freely, the entire town appeared to be deserted.

"What's happening?" he asked. "Where did everybody go?"

"Eventually the truce broke down," the girl explained. "For centuries, all-out war between the humans and the wolves had been averted. Perhaps that was always going to fail, or perhaps the balance could have been saved if only certain people had made the right decisions."

Aghast, Robert turned to her again.

"People need strong leaders," she continued. "They need good, wise leaders. When they don't have that, the whole world can fall apart very quickly."

"I need to find John Tench," Robert replied.

"We have to do something!"

"There's still time for that," she told him. "What you're seeing now is a vision of a possible future, a *likely* future, but it can still be averted. My grandfather worries that his heirs will let everything come crashing down, and that this was is inevitable. The point of no return has almost arrived."

"Stop talking in riddles!" Robert snapped. "What kind of -"

Suddenly hearing a cry of pain, he turned to see a woman running from behind the diner. Two wolves were already in hot pursuit, and one of the creatures caught up to her quickly, dragging her down so that he and his companion could start tearing at her body.

"That's Jessie!" Robert said, taking a step forward. "She works at the diner, she -"

In that moment, he saw one of the wolves ripping the side of the woman's neck away, sending blood splattering across the ground. Trying desperately to crawl away, Jessie let out another wail of pain as she attempted to haul herself up, but the second wolf was already tugging frantically on her left arm, quickly ripping it away from her shoulder.

"Stop that!" Robert yelled, hurrying across the parking lot, waving his stick in an attempt to scare the wolves away. "For God's sake, leave her alone!"

He hit one of the wolves with the end of the stick; the beast turned and snarled at him, but Robert took the chance to poke the animal's side. This forced the wolf back a little, but only by a few paces. Robert turned and struck the other wolf, which was already biting hard on the side of Jessie's chest, yet already the other wolf had returned to renew its attack. For a few seconds Robert could only flail furiously at both animals, aware that he was achieving nothing but unable to leave Jessie at the mercy of the two bloodthirsty creatures. Finally, pulling back, he slipped and fell, landing hard on the ground and watching helplessly as Jessie turned to him.

"Please," she sobbed, "I only -"

One of the wolves pulled hard on the side of her neck, ripping her throat, and then with one final tug began to tear her head clean away from her shoulders.

"Stop!" Robert shouted, reaching for his stick but finding that it had fallen too far away. "Why are you doing this?"

"They're doing it because they're the dominant species here now."

Turning, Robert saw that the little girl was standing nearby, watching impassively as the wolves continued to pull Jessie's lifeless corpse apart.

"In some ways, they always were," she

continued. "They always believed that they were holding back, that they could assert their power if necessary. It looks like they were right."

***

"What the hell is this madness all about?" Robert gasped, stepping into the pitch-black entrance hallway of McGinty's, then turning and pushing the door shut.

Breathless and in pain, having long since lost his stick, he peered out through the dirty little glass window in the door, and he saw several wolves making their way past. The entire town had become almost a battlefield, with the last remaining humans seemingly engaged in a desperate and doomed battle with packs of roaming wolves. Somehow he'd managed to reach the bar, but Robert felt sure that sooner or later the wolves would find their way inside, and he knew deep down that he wouldn't be able to fight them off.

"Do you see now?"

Startled, he spun round and looked into the darkness. He blinked several times, but he was still unable to see anything at all, even if he'd already recognized the voice.

"This is how it ends," the girl continued. "In blood and violence and death. Even for the wolves, there will be consequences. Do you think other humans won't hear what happened here? Do you think they won't come with bigger guns? In the end, nobody will win this war."

"Is this really happening?" Robert asked.

"It *will* really happen," she told him, "if something doesn't change soon. My grandfather's calming presence is gone now, and all that remains are his three sons. Their generation was supposed to fix everything, but instead they're going to make it ten thousand times worse. Even now, the pieces are moving into position and time is running out."

"I don't know what you want me to do," he stammered.

"I want you to warn the others," she explained. "I'll try too, in my own way, but they won't listen to me. You're a respected member of the community, which means your words will carry more weight. I know what you did to my mother, but you have a chance to redeem yourself."

"Your mother?"

Feeling his heart pounding in his chest, Robert continued to stare in the darkness. After a few seconds, he began to make out the faintest hint of the little girl staring back at him.

"You burned her mind," the girl said darkly. "You were only doing what you were told to do, but you could have refused. I'm sure you knew it was wrong. Even when you met her here in Sobolton, you hid the shame of your past. It was just a coincidence that you went all the way to Lakehurst, only to find a girl from *this* town in your treatment room. That, however, is where the coincidence ends. Everything since that moment has been part of the disaster that might lead this town to ruin."

"I'm sorry," he replied, as tears filled his eyes. "I didn't mean..."

He paused for a moment.

"But how can Lisa Sondnes be your mother?" he asked cautiously. "You're only eight or nine years old, and she disappeared twenty years ago."

He waited, but he heard no answer.

"None of this makes sense," he added, struggling to keep from panicking. "I must be having some kind of psychotic breakdown. That's the only possible explanation, I must be imagining all of this, it's some kind of... catastrophic stroke or..." His voice trailed off as he tried to think of the various possibilities. "Or I'm dying," he whispered, "and this is what I'm experiencing as all my neurons fire off for the last time." He began to slide down onto the floor. "This must be what it's like for everyone when they die, they descend into some kind of manic -"

Suddenly he felt the girl's hand touching his.

"You're not dying," she told him, her voice sounding so much closer now. "At least... not yet."

In that moment, hearing wolves snarling on

the other side of the door, Robert could only scream.

***

Suddenly he sat up and found himself outside again, in the street near the edge of the forest. He looked all around, and he quickly spotted two figures slumped on the ground nearby.

Crawling closer, he turned one of the figures over and saw that Tommy's bandages were still missing, exposing the bloodied empty eye sockets. For a few seconds he felt certain that Tommy had to be dead, until finally he heard a faint murmur escaping from the man's lips.

"It's going to be alright," Robert said, before turning as he heard a sobbing sound coming from nearby. "I'm going to get you some help and then -"

Before he could finish, he saw the little girl sitting up. She looked around, as if dazed, and then as she turned to Robert she seemed absolutely terrified, with tears filling her eyes.

"Help me," she sobbed. "Please, you have to help me! Where's my mom?"

CHAPTER TWENTY-FIVE

Twenty years earlier...

"IT'S GOING TO BE fine," Michael said, standing at the window of the cabin and looking out at the large wolf's moonlit corpse. "I don't know how, but... I'm going to fix all of it. I don't know how, but I'll find a way."

He took a deep breath as he tried to find some sense of calm in his troubled mind.

"I'll find a -"

Hearing a bumping sound, he turned and looked across the room. As candlelight flickered against one side of his face, he watched as Lisa tried yet again to sit up. Bound and gagged, she struggled for a few more seconds before freezing as soon as she realized that she'd attracted his attention.

"There's no need to be scared," he told her, before making his way over. "I only did this for your own good. You have to realize that. Right now you're panicking because you're moving from one world to another. To be honest, I'd be more worried if you were finding everything easy." He crouched down in front of her, causing her to immediately pull back as far as she could manage into the corner. "I want to untie you," he continued, "but you have to promise first that you won't do anything stupid. We're on the verge right now of getting everything we've ever wanted, but you have to trust that I know what's best for both of us. Can you do that?"

She stared back at him with terrified eyes, before slowly nodding.

"Are you sure?" he asked.

She nodded again.

"Don't make me regret this," he continued, reaching out and carefully pulling the gag away. "You *have* to trust that I know exactly what I'm doing."

He waited, but even with her mouth now uncovered Lisa merely glared back at him.

"I see such fear in your eyes," he said mournfully, reaching out to touch the side of her face before hesitating as he saw her flinch. "Even though I understand why it's there, it's so hard to know that I'm a tiny part of the cause. You've been through so much, Lisa. Do you know how hard it was for me to let that disgusting pig Joe Hicks just walk away from here, after everything he did to you? I wanted to tear that bastard apart, but I let him go because I know the value of restraint. If I just acted purely on my emotions all the time, I'd be no better than some... common beast."

Again he waited, and again Lisa said nothing.

"I'm not a common beast," he added. "I hope you understand that. Even if I have a beast within, I'm keeping it all suppressed and hidden away." Managing a faint smile, he reached up and touched one side of his own cracked and bleeding face. "Which isn't easy. I hope you didn't just love me for my looks before, Lisa, because... they're long gone."

This time, after waiting for a few more seconds, he reached around her and started loosening the ropes he'd earlier tied around her wrists.

"I'm doing this because I want you to understand that I have our best interests at heart," he explained. "I just want to fix everything, and when we come out the other side you're going to see that it's all been for the best. We're going to be so happy together, Lisa, and we're going to have such an amazing time once everything has settled again. You know what I am now, don't you? Despite all my attempts to avoid this very thing, I've still ended up as the king of my people. I'm sure there'll be some resentment about that, but what's done is done. I'm going to do things very differently."

He pulled the last of the ropes aside and got to his feet, gesturing for her to stand as well.

"My father, and those who ruled before him, had some very old-fashioned ideas. I'm going to shake it all up. Believe me, the future's looking brighter than ever. For you, for me, for the forest and for all the wolves." He paused. "And especially for the town of Sobolton."

He held out his hand.

"Let me help you up," he added.

He waited.

"Please."

He waited again.

"Lisa, don't be like this," he continued, before letting out a labored sigh. "You're just wasting time. Trust me, you're going to come round to my way of seeing things eventually. So why drag it all out? Why not start to become happy right now?"

She hesitated, and then finally she began to get up. Michael moved his hand closer, but she deliberately ignored his offer of help as she stood, and then as she looked around she still seemed wary. Even terrified.

"So aren't you going to congratulate me?" Michael asked with a smile. "You heard what I said just now, didn't you? My father's dead and – whether I like it or not – I'm the new king."

She turned to him.

"I'm the king, Lisa," he added. "That makes you my queen."

"Queen?"

"And so much more," he continued, stepping closer and taking her hands, then holding them up and squeezing tight. "There's so much I haven't told you, because until this moment I never truly believed that it would happen. I've fought against my destiny, Lisa, but now I see that I was fighting the wrong battle. I could never avoid becoming king, because as the oldest son I had no choice. What I *can* avoid, however, is becoming a king like my father, or like his father before him. I can bring about real change."

"I feel like... my head's about to explode," she replied.

"I get it," he said, offering another smile,

"and to be honest, you're dealing with this better than I ever could have hoped. It'll take a long time for both of us to get used to this new reality, but we'll manage. We have each other, and that means we can get through anything that life throws at us." He paused, looking deep into her eyes. "Lisa, this is a fresh start," he added finally. "This is day one of the rest of our lives. You have to understand that."

"You killed your father?"

"Forget about him. He's irrelevant now."

"Your brothers -"

"My brothers have to follow me now," he said, interrupting her. "They have to get their acts together and recognize that I'm in charge, and if they won't... I guess I'll have to make them see the truth. I'm sure they're shocked by what I did to our father, but they'll get used to it." He squeezed her hands tighter still. "But I promise you one thing, Lisa. Anyone who dares to stand in our way, and in the way of our happiness, will regret their actions. I will crush them to dust and make a paste of their bones. I will burn their souls out of existence. I will hang their memories in a gallery of frost and ice, and then I'll crush any sign of them that still remains in this world."

"What does that even mean?" she asked.

"It doesn't matter," he said firmly, "because

we're together now."

Suddenly he pulled her close, hugging her tight. She hesitated, still feeling utterly bewildered, before slowly putting her arms around him. Something about the entire situation felt so very strange, and she wasn't sure that she could ever get used to this new side of Michael.

"My job," she said after a moment. "I have to go back to the town and -"

"You don't need your job. Not now."

"But they need me," she replied. "They're relying on me. I -"

"You live out here now," he continued, "with me. You can't keep going back and forth. I'm sure the people of Sobolton will get used to not having you there. You're not the only veterinarian in the world, Lisa. They'll find someone else, and meanwhile you'll be out here living as my queen, and together we'll rule over the entire forest. I'll make you one more promise, though." Pulling back, he looked deep into her eyes again, and for a moment he seemed to be searching for something. "One day, I will bring our worlds together. I don't know how, and I don't know when, but I'll change everything. Just for you. I'll turn both our world upside down if that's what it takes. For you."

"I'm not sure that's quite what I want," she

told him.

"You'll see," he replied, pulling her close and hugging her tight again. Almost too tight. "This is what we've both always dreamed of, Lisa. Our life together is going to be perfect. Just you and me. Together. Forever."

"Right," she whispered, already staring across the cabin and watching the closed door, and thinking of the moonlit forest beyond. "I mean... I think so."

CHAPTER TWENTY-SIX

Today...

STILL MAKING HIS WAY through the forest, and too stubborn just now to admit that he was lost, John struggled to hold the flashlight in his damaged hands. His broken fingers were burning with pain; he'd just about managed to find a way to keep the flashlight pointing ahead, even if he felt as if he was on the verge of dropping it at all times. Finally, as he stumbled on a root, the flashlight tipped from his hands and hit the ground, quickly rolling down a shallow incline and coming to a rest near another tree.

"Great," John muttered, starting to pick his way down the incline, taking care to not fall again.

Reaching the bottom, he got down onto his

knees. He held out his damaged hands and saw that several of the fingers remained bent in unnatural directions, with the skin already starting to turn a dark shade of purple in places. He had no idea how bad the damage had truly become, but he knew he was going to need medical attention when he finally returned to Sobolton. He took a deep breath, preparing himself for more pain, and then he began to reach down for the flashlight, only to freeze as he heard a faint snarling sound coming from nearby.

Looking past the flashlight, he felt a tightening sense of dread in his chest as he saw the one-eyed wolf glaring at him from just a few feet away.

"Easy now," John said, swallowing hard as he realized that this time he was truly defenseless. Worse, he figured that the wolf would have picked up on that fact already. "I'm not here to hurt you."

He held his hands up a little higher, showing the wolf his cradle of broken fingers.

"See? I don't know if you can understand me on some level, but I have a strange feeling that maybe you can. So I'm going to proceed on that basis. My name is John Tench and I'm the sheriff round here, and all I want to do is maintain order. You get that, right? I'm sure you like order too. I'm only out here to catch the man who put one of my deputies in the hospital, and for better or for worse I've done that now. I need to get back to town and organize a search party to come and retrieve his body. Other than that, I don't want to interfere with whatever's out here. Do we have a deal?"

The wolf's snarl became a little louder, and thick saliva glistened as the creature bared its fangs.

"So I'm going to reach for my flashlight," John added, "and then I'm going to get to my feet, and then I *think* I know which way to go, to get back to the road and eventually reach the town. That means there's no reason for you and I to fall out."

He paused, but he knew he had to make his move. Slowly, he reached toward the flashlight, confident that he'd managed to get through to the wolf and -

Suddenly the beast snarled and lunged at him, biting John's hand and pushing him back, then releasing its grip on him and stepping onto his chest. Letting out a gasp of pain, John looked up and saw the wolf opening its mouth in the moonlight, and in that instant he realized that he was about to die. He braced for the inevitable, for the wolf to bite down again, and he couldn't help but think that he was going to face the same awful fate as Joe Hicks. And then, at the last moment, the wolf seemed to hesitate as more howls rang out in the distance.

Tilting its head, the wolf looked away from John, watching the nearby trees as the howls continued.

John held his breath, too scared to even move, until finally the wolf stepped over him and let out a grunt as it began to walk away. Rolling onto his side, John watched as the creature slipped between two trees. After a few seconds the wolf turned and looked back at him, and John saw a hint of pure hatred in the animal's one remaining eye. For a moment the pair of them simply stared at one another, until eventually the wolf grunted again and turned, quickly running off into the forest and disappearing into the night.

"What the hell?" John stammered, barely able to believe that he'd survived the encounter.

In the distance, more howls filled the night air. In that moment, John began to believe that every wolf in the entire forest was joining the chorus.

***

A few minutes later – or an hour, perhaps, since he'd lost all track of time – John stumbled and almost fell against a tree as he continued to make his way through the forest. In that moment, he found himself wondering just how much time he'd spent wandering lost in the forest since he'd first arrived in Sobolton.

Stopping, he took a moment to get his breath back. He'd found another way to cradle the flashlight, minimizing the pain a little, although when he looked down at his hand he saw the wolf's bite had torn away some flesh around the base of his thumb. He was starting to worry now that his hands were damaged beyond the point of repair, and that they might never function properly again, but he quickly told himself to put those fears out of his mind. For now, he understood finally, he had a bigger problem.

He was completely lost.

As he looked around, he saw no landmarks, no familiar sights, just trees stretching away in every direction. He was shivering a little, and he knew he'd lost some blood, and he began to wonder whether he might be about to collapse. He wasn't a man given to long periods of self-reflection, but he couldn't help thinking that this would be a miserable way to die. For a moment he thought of his own body rotting on the ground, perhaps going undiscovered for months and months; eventually he'd be found, half-eaten by the local wildlife, most likely only identified thanks to his badge still fixed to what remained of his uniform. And after just a short time in the job, he wouldn't really be missed by many people in Sobolton. Robert Law would perhaps raise a glass in his memory, but that'd be about the extent of the mourning.

As for his son...

"No-one cares about you," he heard a voice

saying, and he turned to see Nick standing nearby. He knew his son wasn't really there, of course, but his brain had managed to spit out a pretty good copy. "You're going to die alone and unloved, and that's no worse than you deserve."

"I -"

"What?" Nick asked, cutting him off. "Are you going to make a speech? Are you going to wrap it all up in style? Do you think an eloquent apology might make you feel better?"

John opened his mouth to reply, but he knew he'd never been very good with words. He also knew that he had no right to expect anyone's love. He desperately wished that he was the kind of person who could explain himself, who could put into words everything he was thinking, but deep down he knew that he had no such ability; deep down, he knew that he was a quiet, stoic kind of guy who preferred to keep his mouth shut. He'd always prided himself on those qualities, and he figured there was no point abandoning them now, even if he was close to death.

"Got nothing to say?" Nick sneered. "Pathetic. You can't even be bothered to tell me you're sorry, or that you love me, or that you admit you made a few mistakes in our relationship. You can't be bothered to admit that you're scared, either, and that you don't want to die. You're just like a rock, or a statue of a man. Not a real man at all. You know that's always been your biggest failing, don't you?"

He took a step closer.

"You never change, Dad," he continued. "You never have, and you never will."

Again John opened his mouth, but in that moment he blinked and the image of Nick was gone. He knew that the real Nick was out there somewhere in the world, probably up to no good, and he told himself that he simply had to keep going and try to get back to the town. Feeling slightly annoyed with himself, he set off again, stumbling between the trees, determined to keep going for as long as his legs would function. He could barely even think now, until finally he emerged at the edge of a large moonlit clearing. Stopping, he looked ahead and blinked a couple more times, trying to make sense of what he was seeing. Two things lay ahead in the clearing, and John furrowed his brow as he tried to work out exactly what he'd discovered.

Ahead of him, the bones of a large animal – perhaps a wolf – lay in the moonlight, and a little further off there stood a small, dark cabin.

CHAPTER TWENTY-SEVEN

Twenty years earlier...

"IT'S HARD TO KNOW where I'm going to start," Michael muttered, pacing back and forth near the cabin's door as the candle burned nearby. "I should have prepared more, but it's okay, I'll figure it out eventually. I just don't want to be anything like my father. I want to start the way I mean to continue."

Barely paying any attention to Michael's words, Lisa opened her backpack and looked down at the contents. This was a backpack she'd first carried to the cabin twenty years ago, back when she was a fresh-faced young girl falling in love for the first time. Michael had saved it, and after all these years she began to take out the items that her younger self had considered so important. One of those items, she soon found, was an old paperback book.

Holding the book up, she saw that it was one of the lurid romance sagas she'd loved all those years earlier. Smiling, she peered at the cover and saw a young girl locked in an embrace with a dashing, muscly figure; she dimly remembered starting this book, and as she flicked through the pages she found the plot coming back to her. The heroine had been in love with a vampire, but so many people had tried to keep her away from him. Reaching the final pages, she scanned the text and found that true love had won out, and that the couple had been together evermore. She knew that her younger self would have loved that ending; even now, she figured that any other ending just wouldn't have felt right.

"What are you doing?"

Startled, she turned to find that Michael was standing close.

"Just looking through this," she stammered, before holding the book up. "Revisiting some things from when I was younger."

"Feeling nostalgic?"

"I guess that might be part of it. Sometimes it's hard to remember what I was like back then, before the treatment at Lakehurst. It feels like a lifetime ago."

"You haven't changed," he told her. "Not

really. You're still the same beautiful girl I fell in love with at first sight."

"I think I need some air," she replied, setting the book down and stepping past Michael, only for him to grab her by the wrist.

"Where are you going?" he asked.

"I told you, I need some air."

"I don't know that it's safe out there," he explained. "Some of the wolves might be lingering. My brother -"

"I won't go far," she said, and now she was the one doing the interrupting. "I promise. I just feel like I'm almost suffocating in this cabin, and I just want to..." Taking a deep breath, she realized that her mind was racing, and after a moment she looked down at her wrist and saw his firm grip. "I just want to get my head straight," she continued, fully aware that she probably sounded rather unconvincing. "So much has happened tonight."

"You've become a queen."

"Exactly," she said with a nervous smile. "That's pretty mind-blowing. I just need to try to get my head around it." She tried to pull her wrist away, but Michael maintained his firm grip. "I really won't be long," she added, trying to hide her growing sense of discomfort. "Michael, please, I just really need to get some fresh air."

"It's cold out there."

"I can handle a little cold," she pointed out,

still waiting for him to let go of her wrist. "You have to understand that this is a lot to take in. Don't worry, I promise I won't go far."

***

As soon as she stepped outside, Lisa felt the panic increasing massively in her chest. She'd hoped that a little air might help her to calm down; instead she felt as if her heart was about to explode.

Once she'd shut the door, she made her way down the steps, stopping to look at the dead wolf that still lay in the clearing. She glanced around, but she saw no sign of any other wolves in the area. When she looked at the corpse again, she thought back to all the madness that had unfolded during the course of the night, and she couldn't shake the sense that she was sinking into something she couldn't quite comprehend.

"I'm the king now," she heard Michael's voice saying, echoing through her thoughts, "and you're my queen."

Looking over her shoulder, she saw him pacing past the window, clearly once again lost in his own deliberations. She was seeing a different side to Michael now, a side that seemed wild and untamed; a side that, if she was being completely honest, scared her a little. She'd been so caught up in the rush of her returning memories, and in the realization that she'd fallen in love with Michael, that she hadn't had time to stop and think about what was happening in the world all around her; she felt like one of the heroines in the books she'd always loved to read, except that the 'happy ever after' part of the story was rapidly turning into a nightmare.

Now, as she stepped past the wolf's corpse and looked at the forest all around, Lisa felt as if she could barely breathe. And in that moment she knew that one thing was certain.

She had to run.

Turning again, she saw that Michael was still busy in the cabin, and she told herself that he'd barely even notice if she hurried away. She had no intention of deserting him forever, but she wanted time to think, and she knew that she'd never get that time if Michael was around. Looking down, she saw a faint red mark around her wrist and she realized that his grip had been far too tight; she'd come to recognize a far more forceful side of Michael, and the last thing she wanted to do was try to argue with that side of him while simultaneously attempting to work out what she really wanted to do next.

She saw him passing the window again, and once he was out of sight she instinctively hurried away, making her way quickly past the edge of the clearing and into the forest. She stopped again, feeling desperately out of breath as sheer panic filled her chest. Although she knew that Michael would be angry when he eventually discovered that she'd left, she told herself that she'd be able to talk him round and that he'd understand that she needed some time alone. After all, despite his anger, he was a decent guy and she knew that they were truly in love with each other.

"I just need to clear my head," she said under her breath. "I just need time to figure out what I'm getting myself into."

Convinced that she could get away before Michael noticed, and that the wolves of the forest would leave her alone now that she was supposed to be their 'queen', she began to hurry through the darkness. She almost slipped several times, but she was fairly sure of the best route and she felt sure that she'd be able to think straight just as soon as she managed to get back to Sobolton. In that moment, all she wanted to do was hide away in her apartment and try to get her head straight, and she knew that soon she'd be able to tell Michael exactly what she thought about everything that had happened.

The faster she ran, the more panicked she felt, but for the next few minutes she simply raced through the dark forest. Finally, however, she stopped as she heard a voice crying out in the distance.

"Lisa!" Michael yelled. "Where are you?"

Now the fear became so much stronger. Barely able to think at all, Lisa ran again, bumping against trees in the darkness as she tried desperately to reach the road. She was losing track of her bearings, and she knew there was a risk that she might get lost, but in that moment she felt an instinctive need to get as far away from Michael as possible. Already she was imagining him pursuing her through the night, perhaps even switching into his wolf form, and that was an image that only forced her to keep running. She bumped against another tree, almost losing her footing, then another and another until finally she had to stop for a few seconds to get her breath back.

Looking around in the darkness, she waited for some hint that Michael might be getting closer, but all she heard was the sound of her own heart pounding in her chest. She took a deep breath, but she already worried that she'd stopped for too long so she took a step forward.

Suddenly a hand reached round from behind, clamping tight over her mouth and pulling her back.

CHAPTER TWENTY-EIGHT

Today...

STEPPING PAST THE ANIMAL bones, John looked down and saw that his first instinct had been right: he was no expert, but he was fairly sure already that the bones had belonged to a dog or – more likely – a wolf.

Still, as he stopped and looked at the bones more closely, he realized that this must have been a huge wolf, larger than any he'd seen before. They were old bones, too, and when he reached down and picked one up he quickly felt that its surface was mottled and damaged, as if it had been out in the open for many years. He set that bone aside and picked up the large, heavy skull; looking into the empty eye-sockets, he tried to imagine how ferocious the beast must have been when it was alive, and a shudder passed through his chest as he wondered how such a massive creature could ever have existed.

Setting the skull down, he turned and made his way toward the cabin. Something about the atmosphere in the clearing sent a shiver down his spine, and he was almost able to ignore the crippling pain in his hands as he reached the steps and looked up at the door. A candle was burning in one of the windows, although the light was starting to fade; still, John could tell that while the cabin looked fairly ramshackle and damaged, it certainly didn't appear to have been abandoned. He glance around, just to make sure that he was alone, and then he walked up the steps and knocked on the door.

"Hello?" he called out.

Silence.

"My name is John Tench," he continued, "and I'm the local sheriff. If there's anyone in there, I'd sure like it if you could come out and talk to me for a moment."

Again, only silence.

"The truth is," he added, "I could use a little assistance. If you have a phone or any other way of contacting the town, I..."

Looking down at his hands, he saw the fingers still twisted at various angles, and the bloody mark where the wolf had bitten his left hand.

"I could certainly use some assistance," he said out loud, even though he was already losing hope that someone might answer. "To be entirely honest with you, I'm pretty lost and I'm not even sure of the way home." He turned and looked across the clearing, and after a moment he spotted a faint glow on the horizon. "Although I guess that must be the town," he said under his breath, "so I should be able to figure it out."

Turning to the door again, he hesitated before reaching out and turning the handle. To his surprise, he found that the door opened easily enough, although the hinges let out a complaining groan.

Stepping into the cabin, John felt a floorboard bend slightly beneath his right foot. The glow from the candle allowed him to see a fairly bare room with just a few items of furniture; the place certainly didn't look as if it was occupied, although the candle was proof that someone must have been around at some point that night. Spotting a set of stairs leading up to the top room, John walked over and shone his flashlight up toward the top, but he was already getting the sense that the cabin was entirely empty.

"Hello?" he called out, just in case. "Is there anybody up there?"

He waited, but all he heard was silence and

he was starting to realize that – while the sight of the cabin had been welcome at first – there was nothing that might actually help him. Looking around again, he saw no sign of a phone or a computer, not even any hint of an electrical supply. There was no obvious kitchen, no food or water as far as he could tell, and he was starting to think that he'd soon have to set off again. Part of him wanted to rest until morning, in the hope that the temperature might rise a little, but another part of him worried that if he went to sleep he might not wake up again.

"Okay," he continued cautiously, "if there's really nobody here then I'm just going to leave and -"

Before he could finish, he spotted a backpack over in the corner, partially hidden behind a chair. He wandered over and pulled the backpack out, and then he tipped the contents onto a table. Some clothes fell out, along with a notebook and pen, and finally a book bumped down onto the pile. Picking the book up, John turned it around and saw that it was one of those crazy paranormal romance novels that he personally had never read in his life; the book was clearly old and well-thumbed, and as he leafed through the pages he found himself wondering where its owner might have gone.

And then, spotting a tag on the side of the backpack, he turned it around and saw a name written neatly in ink.

"Lisa Sondnes," he read out loud, and a shudder of recognition immediately rippled through his chest.

He looked around again, and now his mind was racing as he realized that he might have come closer than ever to finding out what had happened twenty years earlier to the town's veterinarian. For some reason that he couldn't quite fathom, Lisa kept popping up in the middle of his other investigations, and although the backpack was clearly old he still felt certain that it had to be relevant somehow.

"Lisa?" he called out. "Lisa Sondnes, are you here? Can you hear me? If you can, I'm Sheriff John Tench and I only want to help you."

He waited, but again – frustratingly – he heard only silence.

"Too easy," he muttered, as he realized that the backpack was perhaps only going to become another piece of a much larger puzzle.

He took a moment to push the items back inside, and then he closed the backpack and looked over at the staircase. Although he'd been planning to leave, now he walked to the stairs and made his way up, but at the top he shone the flashlight all around and saw only a large empty space.

"Not here either," he said under his breath. "So much for that idea."

Once he was satisfied that there was nothing

else left to discover, John headed back down while making a mental note to lead a full team out to check the cabin later. He wanted to turn the place upside down and search for any hint of a further connection to Lisa, but for now he knew he had to get home. Hauling the backpack over his shoulder, he walked back over to the door and stepped outside.

And then, hearing a scrambling thud, he froze at the top of the steps.

He turned and looked back into the cabin. The sound had stopped again, but he had no doubt whatsoever that it had come from somewhere inside. Stepping back into the room, he looked around once more, convinced this time that he wasn't alone. He almost called out, but at the last moment he reminded himself that he might merely scare away whoever was lurking in the cabin. Figuring that he had to be smarter, he continued to look around until he realized that he could see a set of lines on the floor; he walked over to get a closer look, and sure enough he found himself staring down at what appeared to be some kind of hatch.

Another shiver ran through his bones.

Crouching down, he ran his fingertips around the hatch's edge. At first he found no obvious way to pull it open, until he managed to locate a slight dip in the wood. He took a moment to adjust his grip, fighting against the pain in his broken fingers; part of him wanted to give up, but deep down he felt an instinctive sense that this hatch had to be covering something important. He managed to push through the pain, and finally he began to slowly lift the hatch up. There were no hinges; rather, the hatch was merely a section of wood that he been cut out of the floor, and John struggled a little with the weight until he was finally able to shift the hatch aside. Stepping back, he took a moment to get his breath back as the pain in his fingers subsided. As soon as he was able to do so, he grabbed the flashlight and tilted the beam until it was shining down into the space beneath the hatch.

Dirt.

Dirt and tree roots.

Seeing nothing of note, John stared into the emptiness for a few seconds and couldn't quite shake a slight sense of disappointment. He wasn't sure what he'd been expecting to find, but he quickly told himself that he could always get a team to examine the space beneath the hatch in the morning. For now, he simply wanted to pull himself together and figure out the quickest way back into the town.

And then, as he turned to walk away, he happened to spot something moving slightly in the dirty pit. He froze, convinced that he had to be wrong, but sure enough the movement continued, as if something was very slowly shifting beneath the mass of soil and roots. Peering closer, John watched as one of the roots moved slightly aside, revealing the living, breathing shape beneath.

CHAPTER TWENTY-NINE

Twenty years earlier...

"NO! MICHAEL, STOP! MICHAEL, don't -"

Before she could finish, Lisa tripped and fell landing hard on the cabin's hard wooden floor. She let out a gasp and immediately tried to get to her feet, only for Michael to grab her by the shoulders and force her back down.

"Michael, you're hurting me!" she hissed. "What's wrong with you?"

"Why did you try to run away from me?" he asked.

"I wasn't running away!"

"You took off into the forest!"

"I just wanted some time and space to think," she stammered, trying not to panic even though she felt she was seeing a whole new side to Michael's personality. "Is that so wrong?"

She waited, and now she could feel his hot breath on the back of her neck.

"You understand why I need time, don't you?" she added.

"I've done all of this for you," he replied.

"Michael -"

"I had a plan," he continued, cutting her off. "I was just going to sit it all out, I was going to ignore my family and let them squabble with each other. Then you showed up and I got dragged back into the real world. You gave me something to live for, Lisa. Something to hope for. I thought you loved me."

"I do."

"I killed my father for you," he added.

"Michael, no," she sobbed, shaking her head and still not daring to try to turn to him. "Don't say that."

"It's true. I could have just ignored him, but I knew he wouldn't leave you alone. None of them would. They don't approve of you, Lisa, and they think you've changed me. They don't want a human to influence the course of events, so they were going to find a way to get rid of you." He paused for a moment. "In their minds, there was only ever going to be one way. When my father showed up here, I knew deep down that there was only one choice. It was either his life or yours."

"I didn't ask you to do any of this!"

"But you made me!" he snapped angrily. "You made me love you!"

"I didn't know that you were caught up in all this," she replied. "When I met you, I thought you were just some strange guy who wasn't really part of society. I thought you were an outsider, like... I mean, I've always been the same way. I thought we were similar, and I thought that was why we got on so well." Again she waited for him to say something, and again she realized she could feel him breathing on the back of her neck. "I had no idea about the rest of it," she added. "The wolves, the world out here in the forest, all this stuff about kings... I had no clue."

"Would you have done things differently if you'd known?"

"I don't know," she replied, before pausing again. "Maybe."

She waited, and this time he let go of her shoulders. Turning, she watched him walking over to the window; as he looked out at the clearing, he seemed more troubled than ever before. Sitting up, Lisa felt herself drawn to the door, but she knew Michael wasn't going to let her go. Not yet.

"You're a queen," he said finally.

"Michael -"

"You're *my* queen," he continued, "and I'm

your king. Okay, we're not married yet, but that was always the plan. And we were going to rule over all of this. My brothers would have had to bow down before us, and if they refused... I'd have given them no choice." He paused. "And I was going to make everything different. I was going to end the divide between the two worlds. I can still do all of that, but Lisa..."

He turned to her.

"I need you by my side."

"I never said I was leaving you," she replied, trying to think of some way to talk herself out of trouble. "I'm sorry I ran, I shouldn't have done that, but I just needed to get away for a while and figure things out in my head. I feel as if I'm on the verge of entering some strange new world and -"

"You are."

"So I need to get used to that!" she added, before slowly getting to her feet and dusting herself down. "I'm on your side, Michael. I just need to understand how everything's going to change."

"You're going to live out here with me."

"In this cabin?"

"There's more to this world than a rundown old cabin," he replied. "As rulers of the forest, we automatically become members of the House of Sangreth. That's the ancient wolf home, it's where our bloodline comes from." He watched her face for a moment, as if he was searching for a particular reaction. "And that doesn't mean anything to you," he added, "because it's a world that has always been hidden from humans."

"I want to learn about it," she told him. "Just... at my own pace."

"It's not something you can venture into slowly," he told her. "Very few humans have ever been to Sangreth, and fewer still have made it back. You're lucky, you have me to guide you, but the journey will still be difficult. It's a journey we have to take eventually, though, because all rulers of this world have to pay tribute. You need to be trained for that moment."

"This is exactly the sort of thing I still need to wrap my head around," she replied, taking a step forward. "I've never heard of Sangreth in my life. You might as well be speaking a foreign language."

"I'm starting to wonder whether my father was right," he said with a sigh. "I might have been asking too much. Perhaps you and I can't be together after all."

"Please don't think like that," she said, struggling once more to hold back tears. "This is the whole reason I ran in the first place, Michael. I know I can deal with everything you're telling me, but occasionally I'm going to have to take time out to think about it." Stepping even closer, she reached out and touched the side of his arm. "I know you have so much to teach me, and I'm eager to learn, but can we try to slow the pace down a little?"

"I looked at one of those books you left here," he replied. "No-one seems to ever slow the pace down in those."

"That's because they're just stories," she suggested. "This is real life."

"You're the only human I could ever consider bringing into this world," he said firmly. "That's because I know how strong you are. Even though we were apart for so long, we've also been together for two decades. I have no doubt whatsoever that you can deal with all of this, so long as I guide you properly. But if you run off, if you act like you're not committed, then you'll make me doubt you."

"That's not what I wanted to do."

She waited for a reply, but she felt now as if she was getting through to him.

"Let's do this properly," she added cautiously. "We'll compromise, and we'll get through it together. We might have to muddle through a few parts of it, but I'm sure we have a lot we can teach each other. We just have to remember that we're in this together." Again she waited for some kind of response. "I guess I can get used to the idea of being a queen eventually. I know it won't be like all those books, but... trial and error might help."

He turned to her, and she could see the doubt in his eyes. A moment later, as if he'd heard something, he suddenly turned and looked toward the window.

"What is it?" she asked.

Hurrying away from her, he looked out once again at the clearing. Lisa followed and looked out as well, but she saw nothing except the corpse of the large wolf glistening out there in the moonlight. She continued to watch for any sign of movement, even as Michael stepped back.

"Are you being jumpy?" she continued. "If -"

Before she could finish, she heard a creaking sound. Turning, she saw that Michael had opened a hatch in the floor; she'd noticed the hatch before, but he'd always insisted that it didn't lead to anything more interesting than a hole in the ground. Now, making her way over, she looked down and saw that he'd been telling the truth. Twisted tree roots filled the space, criss-crossing the dark and dirty space.

"I always swore that I'd keep you safe," Michael whispered. "I have to stick to my word, at least until I can be certain that they'll all leave you alone."

"I think I can handle myself pretty well," she suggested, managing a faint smile.

"You can't," he said firmly. "Not in this

world."

"I'm still here, aren't I?"

"Don't get cocky," he replied, scowling at her. "It's a miracle you're still alive, but we can't rely on miracles forever. I have two very angry brothers out there right now, and at least one of them is going to want to prove a point. I can't deal with them while also watching over you. It's impossible."

"Now you're sounding so serious again," she told him, before stepping forward and looking more closely at the hole in the floor. "I'm starting to think that I need to take some kind of Werewolf 101 class. I guess nothing like that exists, huh? But is there any kind of book I can read that might help? What about a history of your people, and this Sangreth place and everything else? Is there some way I can quickly get up to speed with all of it?"

"There are no shortcuts," he said darkly. "No compromises."

"Then you'll have to be my teacher," she suggested, hoping that he might come around to her way of seeing things. "You can give me lessons."

"I'm sorry, Lisa," he replied, "but it isn't going to work like that. You can't compromise in a world you don't understand, and you're already in some much danger." He reached around from behind, putting his hands on the sides of her arms and then leaning close to her right ear. "I'm going to have to take charge and keep you safe, at least for now. You might not understand why I do what I do, not yet, but eventually you'll see that I have no choice."

"What exactly does that mean?" she asked, before waiting a few seconds for him to reply. "Michael?"

He gripped her arms tighter.

"You're scaring me," she added.

"I have to protect you," he hissed. "I protected you from that bastard at the motel, and now I'm going to protect you from everyone else."

"The motel?" She paused as a ripple of dread ran through her chest. "What did you do at the motel?"

"I had no choice," he sneered. "What was his name again? Wade? He was no good for you, Lisa. He was getting in the way."

"Did you kill him?" she asked, and now her voice was trembling with fear. "Michael, did you kill Wade?"

"I'm so sorry, Lisa," he replied firmly, "but I have to hide you away until it's safe for you to come out. I know you won't agree to that, so there's really only one way this is ever going to work."

CHAPTER THIRTY

Today...

"WHAT THE HELL IS going on in this place?" Robert Law snapped angrily, holding the little girl's hand as he stepped out of the elevator and looked across the ward at Middleford Cross Hospital. "Have you all lost our goddamn minds?"

"There you are!" Garrett gasped, hurrying away from the desk and making his way over. "Doctor Law, I've been trying to get hold of you for -"

"Are you aware," Robert sneered, cutting him off, "that one of your patients has been wandering around the town tonight?"

"I -"

"I just had to get Tommy Wallace brought

back here in an ambulance," he continued through gritted teeth. "That man was close to death when I left earlier, and now he's in an even worse way. You're going to be lucky if I don't have your license suspended for this!"

"Tommy vanished and -"

"I don't want to hear excuses!" Robert shouted, reaching out and shoving Garrett hard in the chest, forcing him to take a step back just as Jessie hurried around the corner. "Get your sorry ass down to the emergency room and see what you can do to help them out. Tommy's in a bad way, he's lost a lot of blood and I'm not sure he's going to make it."

Garrett immediately hurried toward the elevator.

"Oh, and if he dies," Robert continued, turning to him, "I'm going to hold you solely responsible. Young man, you have no idea how much trouble I can cause for you, but I'll end your career in a flash. I'll make sure you can't even get hired as a hospital janitor!"

"I'll... go right now," Garrett replied. "I'll do whatever I can to help."

Robert watched as he hurried through the double doors, and then he turned to see that Jessie was watching with a shocked expression.

"And don't think you're out of the woods either!" he told her. "What kind of operation are you people running here, anyway?"

"I'm sorry," Jessie replied, before stepping closer and looking down at the girl. "Hey, are you okay?"

"Of course she's not okay!" Robert hissed. "Do you think *anyone's* okay tonight? Have you heard anything from Sheriff John Tench?"

"Not that I'm aware of."

"I need a goddamn phone," Robert muttered, letting go of the girl's hand. "I feel like the entire world's falling apart around me tonight. Can you look after this girl for a few minutes?" Without waiting for an answer, he limped over to the desk and grabbed the phone's receiver. "You can't rely on anyone these days. If you want something doing, you have to do it yourself!"

"Sweetheart, hey," Jessie said softly, crouching down and looking into the girl's eyes. "How are you doing? Shall we get you cleaned up?"

The girl hesitated, before nodding slightly.

"Honey, what's your name?" Jessie asked.

The girl hesitated again, and then she glanced around as if she was worried that she might be overheard. When she turned to Jessie again, the fear was clear in her eyes.

"Eloise," she whispered finally. "My name's Eloise. Do you know where I can find my mom?"

"I don't," Jessie told her, "but you can tell me as much as you know, and we'll track her down somehow. First, though, why don't you come through to one of the examination rooms and we'll clean you up properly. Does that sound like a good idea?"

Eloise thought about that for a moment, and then she nodded again.

"Okay, let's go," Jessie said, taking her by the hand and leading her into a nearby room. "You look like you've been a brave girl tonight. Do you want to tell me what's been happening?"

"Madness," Robert snapped, unable to contain a sense of anger as he set the receiver down, having failed to get through to John. He paused, before dialing again. "This whole world has gone insane. We've got dead girls getting up and walking around, we've got deputies with their eyes gouged out, we've got visions of wolves ripping people apart in the streets. What's next?" The lights flickered as he heard his call going straight through to John's voicemail. "Damn it, Tench, where are you?"

"Right here."

Startled, Robert spun around. Seeing John stepping out of the elevator, he opened his mouth to ask what the hell was going on, and then he froze as he saw that John was holding a naked, unconscious woman in his arms.

"I found her in a cabin in the forest," John said, barely able to get the words out as he struggled to stay on his feet. "I think it's Lisa Sondnes."

***

"She's stable for now," Robert said a short while later, looking through the window and watching as several nurses worked on Lisa in the examination room. "She hasn't woken up yet. We don't know what's wrong with her, but based on her appearance right now I'd guess... a lot."

He paused, before turning to John.

"How exactly did you find her again?"

"She was in some kind of space beneath the cabin floor," John explained, keeping his eyes fixed on Lisa's bedraggled figure. Thick, unruly graying hair still covered most of her face, although after a moment some of that hair was pulled aside by one of the nurses. "She was barely alive. I think she was trying to hide from me."

"It's been twenty years," Robert replied. "She's been missing since..."

His voice trailed off for a moment.

"You need to get checked over," he added.

"I'm fine."

"You're clearly not fine," Robert pointed out, looking him up and down. "What happened to your hands? Your fingers -"

"I'll get that looked at later," John said firmly. "Right now, I need to speak to Lisa as soon as she wakes up." He turned to Robert. "And the girl. You said Eloise, the girl from the ice... how can she have woken up?"

"Beats me," Robert replied, "but she's getting cleaned up by one of the team right now."

"She's dead."

"I know that."

"You performed an autopsy on her."

"I know that too!" Robert hissed angrily. "Do you not think I'm aware of that fact? I know you've had a crazy night, John, but I've seen a few things as well. I'll fill you in on the details later, but let's just say... I really don't think I have a good grip on what's going on around here."

"Everything is coming crashing together," John whispered.

"What did you say?"

"Nothing," John added, before shaking his head. "I don't want any word of this getting out. Not yet, at least. Not about Lisa, and not about the girl... Eloise... I want it kept between us and the medical staff. Do you think that's possible?"

"Word'll get out sooner rather than later," Robert suggested. "You've probably got a few hours at most."

"Then that'll have to do," John said, turning his attention back to Lisa. Most of the hair had been pulled aside from her face now, revealing the features of a desperately thin and obviously malnourished woman who looked almost like a corpse. "This has to all be connected. I saw things tonight, Robert. I saw things that part of me knows can't be possible, yet I saw them with my own two eyes. Ever since I arrived in Sobolton, I've been struggling to deny what's going on in this town. And out in that forest. I don't think I can deny it now."

"Join the club," Robert muttered, before pausing for a moment. "I'm going to go and check on Eloise, then I'm going to see what's going on with Lisa, and *then* I'm afraid I'll have to insist on taking a look at your hands. You're not going to be any use to anyone if you can't use them, John."

"Fine," John replied, narrowing his gaze a little as he watched Lisa getting hooked up to some equipment. "Do what you need to do. So will I."

"I've never known a night like this one," Robert said as he turned and limped away along the corridor. "Sometimes I think I might have just lost my mind. I mean, that'd be the simplest explanation, wouldn't it? I've lost my mind and none of this is real."

He was still talking to himself as he disappeared around the corner.

Having barely noticed anything his friend had told him, John continued to watch as the team worked on Lisa. Staring at her face, he felt certain that if – no, when – she woke up, she'd be able to tell him a whole lot about the forest, and about the girl, and about everything that had been happening in and around Sobolton. Part of him wanted to rush into the room and grab her, to shake her awake and force her to talk while she was still alive. He knew there was a chance she might never wake up at all, but he told himself that he hadn't come this close to the truth only to fail at the last moment. The more he watched her, the more he felt sure that he needed to talk to Lisa Sondnes at the earliest possible chance.

His injured hands hung down at his sides. Several of the fingers were twisted and broken. A nasty wound had been left by the bite of one of the wolves. Already, the wolf's saliva was penetrating deeper and deeper into John's body, coursing through his veins, mixing with – and slowly starting to change – his blood.

EPILOGUE

SEVERAL HOURS LATER, CAROLYN set her notebook on the table and made her way to the coffee machine in the break-room. Exhausted from a night spent fielding calls, she still had no idea what was actually going on; she knew that Sheriff Tench was at the hospital, along with Doctor Law, and that something had happened. She just didn't know what.

All she *did* know was that she desperately needed coffee.

After setting her mug under the spout, she pressed the button on the side of the machine and waited while the water began to heat up. Almost too exhausted to even think, she told herself that she was going to have to keep going on coffee alone, and that there'd be no chance to slip home and take a nap. Not that she wanted to leave her post, anyway; for Carolyn, working for the local sheriff was as much an honor as a job, and she knew that the team would need her to keep everything running behind the scenes. As the coffee machine began to hum, she told herself that – as usual – she was simply going to have to find some way to keep going.

"You can do this," she said under her breath. "You just -"

Suddenly the machine's spout tilted upward. Before Carolyn could react, coffee sprayed out of the machine and splattered against the front of her shirt.

"What the -"

Stepping back, she looked down at the liquid that was now soaking through the shirt's fabric. She stepped around the stream and tilted the spout back down, and then she turned and punched the door of a nearby cupboard, succeeding only in hurting her own fist.

"Damn it!" she sobbed, unable to hold back the tears any longer. Turning, she hurried out of the room. "Why does this always have to happen to me? And why now?"

Once the room had been left empty, the machine continued to rumble for a few seconds, filling the mug with the rest of the coffee. Finally the system powered down, leaving the steaming mug standing on a metal plate. The top of the machine was made of metal too, and this metal reflected not only a distorted view of the room, but also a faint hint of a human face that could be seen nowhere else.

"Huh," the voice of Joe Hicks muttered darkly, with more than a hint of amusement. "I *told* you things'd go to crap as soon as I was gone."

***

"That's not what I heard," Wendy said, leaning against the counter in the diner with her phone against one side of her face. "I can't really say too much, we've got a customer right now but..."

She turned and looked toward the table at the far end, where a man sat with his breakfast. She didn't know the man, he certainly wasn't a regular at the diner, but she knew she couldn't be caught gossiping.

"Okay," she continued, turning and heading over to the service hatch, while lowering her voice as she continued to speak into the phone, "what I heard is that something major went down at the hospital."

She listened for a moment as her friend Merris spoke on the other end of the line.

"Yeah, Middleford Cross," she added. "I don't know what it was all about, but there were loads of police cruisers out there this morning when I passed on my way to work. And I saw a couple of cruisers heading out to the forest, so I figure that has to be connected somehow as well. But here's the real crazy thing... I didn't see any sign of the new sheriff, which seems strange since you'd think he'd be right at the center of it all."

She listened again.

"Sure," she continued, "he *might* have been inside the hospital already. I guess that's true. But don't you think it's strange that there's been no official statement? Not a word. I've checked all their socials, and the office hasn't so much as mentioned a damn thing. It's just a load of automated messages about the usual stuff no-one cares about."

Standing on tip-toes for a moment, she saw that the strange man was still eating his breakfast.

"So something's going down," she said, her voice tight with tension. "I sent a text to Carolyn, but she hasn't replied. And that's unusual in itself, because she's usually really quick to give us all the gossip. Mark my words, Merris, something major happened during the night and I for one can't wait to find out what it is. And that's before you even get to the whole Tommy Wallace thing, because Linda spoke to Bryce and Bryce said she ran into Tracy Wallace and apparently she's in an absolutely terrible state. I think Tommy's hurt way more than any of us realized. I think his injuries might be life-threatening. Certainly life-changing, at least."

Listening as Merris discussed some other theories, Wendy looked across the diner again and saw that the strange man was getting to his feet and preparing to head to the door.

"I need to go," she said, interrupting Merris. "I'll call you back in two minutes, okay? Just hold that thought!"

Once she'd cut the call, she hurried to the counter and saw that the man was almost at the door. He'd paid his tab after ordering, which she'd found unusual, so she had no reason to say anything to him; at the same time, there was something handsome and slightly roguish about the guy, and these were qualities that had always appealed to Wendy. Deep down she knew there was no real point trying to start a conversation, yet she'd always enjoyed harmlessly flirting with customers.

"Everything alright?"

"Fine, thank you," he replied as he opened the door.

"So you're new in town, huh?" she continued. "Or just passing through?"

"Oh, I'm from around here," the man said, stopping for a moment before turning to her, once again revealing the patch over his missing left eye. "I don't get into town much these days," he added. "I'm just here to deal with some family business."

THE HORRORS OF SOBOLTON

1. Little Miss Dead
2. Swan Territory
3. Dead Widow Road
4. In a Lonely Grave
5. Electrification
6. Man on the Moon
7. Cry of the Wolf

More titles coming soon!

Next in this series

CRY OF THE WOLF
(THE HORRORS OF SOBOLTON BOOK 7)

Now that he's finally solved one of the biggest mysteries in Sobolton's history, John Tench is about to find out that his troubles are only just beginning. While Lisa Sondnes fights for her life in a hospital room, dark forces are starting to emerge from the forest with only one thing in mind.

Revenge.

Michael might be out of the picture for now, but his brother believes that their people have been too forgiving for too long. Convinced that the people of Sobolton have ignored the agreement that was struck many years earlier, the brother is determined to avoid repeating the mistakes made by his father. And if that means drawing blood, then so be it.

John, however, has another problem brewing in his own bones. Although he might not want to admit the truth, he sustained an injury out in the forest, and now that injury is starting to make itself felt. Can he fight to save himself, or is he about to discover the horrifying truth that led – many years earlier – to the town's foundation?

AMY CROSS

Also by Amy Cross

1689
(The Haunting of Hadlow House book 1)

All Richard Hadlow wants is a happy family and a peaceful home. Having built the perfect house deep in the Kent countryside, now all he needs is a wife. He's about to discover, however, that even the most perfectly-laid plans can go horribly and tragically wrong.

The year is 1689 and England is in the grip of turmoil. A pretender is trying to take the throne, but Richard has no interest in the affairs of his country. He only cares about finding the perfect wife and giving her a perfect life. But someone – or something – at his newly-built house has other ideas. Is Richard's new life about to be destroyed forever?

Hadlow House is brand new, but already there are strange whispers in the corridors and unexplained noises at night. Has Richard been unlucky, is his new wife simply imagining things, or is a dark secret from the past about to rise up and deliver Richard's worst nightmare? Who wins when the past and the present collide?

Also by Amy Cross

The Haunting of Nelson Street
(The Ghosts of Crowford book 1)

Crowford, a sleepy coastal town in the south of England, might seem like an oasis of calm and tranquility. Beneath the surface, however, dark secrets are waiting to claim fresh victims, and ghostly figures plot revenge.

Having finally decided to leave the hustle of London, Daisy and Richard Johnson buy two houses on Nelson Street, a picturesque street in the center of Crowford. One house is perfect and ready to move into, while the other is a fire-ravaged wreck that needs a lot of work. They figure they have plenty of time to work on the damaged house while Daisy recovers from a traumatic event.

Soon, they discover that the two houses share a common link to the past. Something awful once happened on Nelson Street, something that shook the town to its core.

Also by Amy Cross

The Revenge of the Mercy Belle
(The Ghosts of Crowford book 2)

The year is 1950, and a great tragedy has struck the town of Crowford. Three local men have been killed in a storm, after their fishing boat the Mercy Belle sank. A mysterious fourth man, however, was rescue. Nobody knows who he is, or what he was doing on the Mercy Belle... and the man has lost his memory.

Five years later, messages from the dead warn of impending doom for Crowford. The ghosts of the Mercy Belle's crew demand revenge, and the whole town is being punished. The fourth man still has no memory of his previous existence, but he's married now and living under the named Edward Smith. As Crowford's suffering continues, the locals begin to turn against him.

What really happened on the night the Mercy Belle sank? Did the fourth man cause the tragedy? And will Crowford survive if this man is not sent to meet his fate?

Also by Amy Cross

The Devil, the Witch and the Whore
(The Deal book 1)

"Leave the forest alone. Whatever's out there, just let it be. Don't make it angry."

When a horrific discovery is made at the edge of town, Sheriff James Kopperud realizes the answers he seeks might be waiting beyond in the vast forest. But everybody in the town of Deal knows that there's something out there in the forest, something that should never be disturbed. A deal was made long ago, a deal that was supposed to keep the town safe. And if he insists on investigating the murder of a local girl, James is going to have to break that deal and head out into the wilderness.

Meanwhile, James has no idea that his estranged daughter Ramsey has returned to town. Ramsey is running from something, and she thinks she can find safety in the vast tunnel system that runs beneath the forest. Before long, however, Ramsey finds herself coming face to face with creatures that hide in the shadows. One of these creatures is known as the devil, and another is known as the witch. They're both waiting for the whore to arrive, but for very different reasons. And soon Ramsey is offered a terrible deal, one that could save or destroy the entire town, and maybe even the world.

Also by Amy Cross

If You Didn't Like Me Then, You Probably Won't Like Me Now

One year ago, Sheryl and her friends did something bad. Really bad. They ritually humiliated local girl Rachel Ritter, before posting the video online for all to see. After that night, Rachel left town and was never seen again. Until now.

Late one night, Sheryl and her friends realize that Rachel's back. At first they think there's on reason to be concerned, but a series of strange events soon convince them that they need to be worried. On the outside, Rachel acts as if all is forgiven, but she's hiding a shocking secret that soon starts to have deadly consequences.

By the time they understand the full horror of Rachel's plans, Sheryl and her friends might be too late to save themselves. Is Rachel really out for revenge? What does she have in store for her tormentors? And just how far is she willing to go? Would she, for example, do something that nobody in all of human history has ever managed to achieve?

If You Didn't Like Me Then, You Probably Won't Like Me Now is a horror novel about the surprising nature of revenge, about the power of hatred, and about the future of humanity.

Also by Amy Cross

The Soul Auction

"I saw a woman on the beach. I watched her face a demon."

Thirty years after her mother's death, Alice Ashcroft is drawn back to the coastal English town of Curridge. Somebody in Curridge has been reviewing Alice's novels online, and in those reviews there have been tantalizing hints at a hidden truth. A truth that seems to be linked to her dead mother.

"Thirty years ago, there was a soul auction."

Once she reaches Curridge, Alice finds strange things happening all around her. Something attacks her car. A figure watches her on the beach at night. And when she tries to find the person who has been reviewing her books, she makes a horrific discovery.

What really happened to Alice's mother thirty years ago? Who was she talking to, just moments before dropping dead on the beach? What caused a huge rockfall that nearly tore a nearby cliff-face in half? And what sinister presence is lurking in the grounds of the local church?

Also by Amy Cross

A House in London

Having recently moved to London, Jennifer Griffith needs a job. Any job. When she spots an advert for a position as a nanny, she immediately applies, but she has no idea that she's about to be drawn into a nightmare.

Arthur and Vivian Diebold are no ordinary couple, and their son Ivan is no ordinary baby. Horrified by what she discovers, Jennifer is persuaded to stay for at least one night, while the Diebolds enjoy a rare moment away from the house. Before the night is over, however, Jennifer starts to realize that this particular house is hiding some very dark secrets.

A House in London is a horror novel about a girl who dreams of success and fortune in London, and about an elderly couple who'll stop at nothing to achieve their goal.

Also by Amy Cross

The Ghost of Molly Holt

"Molly Holt is dead. There's nothing to fear in this house."

When three teenagers set out to explore an abandoned house in the middle of a forest, they think they've found the location where the infamous Molly Holt video was filmed.

They've found much more than that...

Tim doesn't believe in ghosts, but he has a crush on a girl who does. That's why he ends up taking her out to the house, and it's also why he lets her take his only flashlight. But as they explore the house together, Tim and Becky start to realize that something else might be lurking in the shadows.

Something that, ten years ago, suffered unimaginable pain.

Something that won't rest until a terrible wrong has been put right.

MAN ON THE MOON

Also by Amy Cross

American Coven

He kidnapped three women and held them in his basement. He thought they couldn't fight back. He was wrong...

Snatched from the street near her home, Holly Carter is taken to a rural house and thrown down into a stone basement. She meets two other women who have also been kidnapped, and soon Holly learns about the horrific rituals that take place in the house. Eventually, she's called upstairs to take her place in the ice bath.

As her nightmare continues, however, Holly learns about a mysterious power that exists in the basement, and which the three women might be able to harness. When they finally manage to get through the metal door, however, the women have no idea that their fight for freedom is going to stretch out for more than a decade, or that it will culminate in a final, devastating demonstration of their new-found powers.

Also by Amy Cross

The Ash House

Why would anyone ever return to a haunted house?

For Diane Mercer the answer is simple. She's dying of cancer, and she wants to know once and for all whether ghosts are real.

Heading home with her young son, Diane is determined to find out whether the stories are real. After all, everyone else claimed to see and hear strange things in the house over the years. Everyone except Diane had some kind of experience in the house, or in the little ash house in the yard.

As Diane explores the house where she grew up, however, her son is exploring the yard and the forest. And while his mother might be struggling to come to terms with her own impending death, Daniel Mercer is puzzled by fleeting appearances of a strange little girl who seems drawn to the ash house, and by strange, rasping coughs that he keeps hearing at night.

The Ash House is a horror novel about a woman who desperately wants to know what will happen to her when she dies, and about a boy who uncovers the shocking truth about a young girl's murder.

Haunted

Twenty years ago, the ghost of a dead little girl drove
Sheriff Michael Blaine to his death.

Now, that same ghost is coming for his daughter.

Returning to the small town where she grew up, Alex
Roberts is determined to live a normal, quiet life. For the
residents of Railham, however, she's an unwelcome
reminder of the town's darkest hour.

Twenty years ago, nine-year-old Mo Garvey was found
brutally murdered in a nearby forest. Everyone thinks
that Alex's father was responsible, but if the killer was
brought to justice, why is the ghost of Mo Garvey still
after revenge?

And how far will the real killer go to protect his secret,
when Alex starts getting closer to the truth?

Haunted is a horror novel about a woman who has to
face her past, about a town that would rather forget, and
about a little girl who refuses to let death stand in her
way.

AMY CROSS

AMY CROSS

BOOKS BY AMY CROSS

1. Dark Season: The Complete First Series (2011)

2. Werewolves of Soho (Lupine Howl book 1) (2012)

3. Werewolves of the Other London (Lupine Howl book 2) (2012)

4. Ghosts: The Complete Series (2012)

5. Dark Season: The Complete Second Series (2012)

6. The Children of Black Annis (Lupine Howl book 3) (2012)

7. Destiny of the Last Wolf (Lupine Howl book 4) (2012)

8. Asylum (The Asylum Trilogy book 1) (2012)

9. Dark Season: The Complete Third Series (2013)

10. Devil's Briar (2013)

11. Broken Blue (The Broken Trilogy book 1) (2013)

12. The Night Girl (2013)

13. Days 1 to 4 (Mass Extinction Event book 1) (2013)

14. Days 5 to 8 (Mass Extinction Event book 2) (2013)

15. The Library (The Library Chronicles book 1) (2013)

16. American Coven (2013)

17. Werewolves of Sangreth (Lupine Howl book 5) (2013)

18. Broken White (The Broken Trilogy book 2) (2013)

19. Grave Girl (Grave Girl book 1) (2013)

20. Other People's Bodies (2013)

21. The Shades (2013)

22. The Vampire's Grave and Other Stories (2013)

23. Darper Danver: The Complete First Series (2013)

24. The Hollow Church (2013)

25. The Dead and the Dying (2013)

26. Days 9 to 16 (Mass Extinction Event book 3) (2013)

27. The Girl Who Never Came Back (2013)

28. Ward Z (The Ward Z Series book 1) (2013)

29. Journey to the Library (The Library Chronicles book 2) (2014)

30. The Vampires of Tor Cliff Asylum (2014)

31. The Family Man (2014)

32. The Devil's Blade (2014)

33. The Immortal Wolf (Lupine Howl book 6) (2014)

34. The Dying Streets (Detective Laura Foster book 1) (2014)

35. The Stars My Home (2014)

36. The Ghost in the Rain and Other Stories (2014)

37. Ghosts of the River Thames (The Robinson Chronicles book 1) (2014)

38. The Wolves of Cur'eath (2014)

39. Days 46 to 53 (Mass Extinction Event book 4) (2014)

40. The Man Who Saw the Face of the World (2014)

41. The Art of Dying (Detective Laura Foster book 2) (2014)

42. Raven Revivals (Grave Girl book 2) (2014)

43. Arrival on Thaxos (Dead Souls book 1) (2014)

44. Birthright (Dead Souls book 2) (2014)

45. A Man of Ghosts (Dead Souls book 3) (2014)

46. The Haunting of Hardstone Jail (2014)

47. A Very Respectable Woman (2015)

48. Better the Devil (2015)

49. The Haunting of Marshall Heights (2015)

50. Terror at Camp Everbee (The Ward Z Series book 2) (2015)

51. Guided by Evil (Dead Souls book 4) (2015)

52. Child of a Bloodied Hand (Dead Souls book 5) (2015)

53. Promises of the Dead (Dead Souls book 6) (2015)

54. Days 54 to 61 (Mass Extinction Event book 5) (2015)

55. Angels in the Machine (The Robinson Chronicles book 2) (2015)

56. The Curse of Ah-Qal's Tomb (2015)

57. Broken Red (The Broken Trilogy book 3) (2015)

58. The Farm (2015)

59. Fallen Heroes (Detective Laura Foster book 3) (2015)

60. The Haunting of Emily Stone (2015)

61. Cursed Across Time (Dead Souls book 7) (2015)

62. Destiny of the Dead (Dead Souls book 8) (2015)

63. The Death of Jennifer Kazakos (Dead Souls book 9) (2015)

64. Alice Isn't Well (Death Herself book 1) (2015)

65. Annie's Room (2015)

66. The House on Everley Street (Death Herself book 2) (2015)

67. Meds (The Asylum Trilogy book 2) (2015)

68. Take Me to Church (2015)

69. Ascension (Demon's Grail book 1) (2015)

70. The Priest Hole (Nykolas Freeman book 1) (2015)

71. Eli's Town (2015)

72. The Horror of Raven's Briar Orphanage (Dead Souls book 10) (2015)

73. The Witch of Thaxos (Dead Souls book 11) (2015)

74. The Rise of Ashalla (Dead Souls book 12) (2015)

75. Evolution (Demon's Grail book 2) (2015)

76. The Island (The Island book 1) (2015)

77. The Lighthouse (2015)

78. The Cabin (The Cabin Trilogy book 1) (2015)

79. At the Edge of the Forest (2015)

80. The Devil's Hand (2015)

81. The 13th Demon (Demon's Grail book 3) (2016)

82. After the Cabin (The Cabin Trilogy book 2) (2016)

83. The Border: The Complete Series (2016)

84. The Dead Ones (Death Herself book 3) (2016)

85. A House in London (2016)

86. Persona (The Island book 2) (2016)

87. Battlefield (Nykolas Freeman book 2) (2016)

88. Perfect Little Monsters and Other Stories (2016)

89. The Ghost of Shapley Hall (2016)

90. The Blood House (2016)

91. The Death of Addie Gray (2016)

92. The Girl With Crooked Fangs (2016)

93. Last Wrong Turn (2016)

94. The Body at Auercliff (2016)

95. The Printer From Hell (2016)

96. The Dog (2016)

97. The Nurse (2016)

98. The Haunting of Blackwych Grange (2016)

99. Twisted Little Things and Other Stories (2016)

100. The Horror of Devil's Root Lake (2016)

101. The Disappearance of Katie Wren (2016)

102. B&B (2016)

103. The Bride of Ashbyrn House (2016)

104. The Devil, the Witch and the Whore (The Deal Trilogy book 1) (2016)

105. The Ghosts of Lakeforth Hotel (2016)

106. The Ghost of Longthorn Manor and Other Stories (2016)

107. Laura (2017)

108. The Murder at Skellin Cottage (Jo Mason book 1) (2017)

109. The Curse of Wetherley House (2017)

110. The Ghosts of Hexley Airport (2017)

111. The Return of Rachel Stone (Jo Mason book 2) (2017)

112. Haunted (2017)

113. The Vampire of Downing Street and Other Stories (2017)

114. The Ash House (2017)

115. The Ghost of Molly Holt (2017)

116. The Camera Man (2017)

117. The Soul Auction (2017)

118. The Abyss (The Island book 3) (2017)

119. Broken Window (The House of Jack the Ripper book 1) (2017)

120. In Darkness Dwell (The House of Jack the Ripper book 2) (2017)

121. Cradle to Grave (The House of Jack the Ripper book 3) (2017)

122. The Lady Screams (The House of Jack the Ripper book 4) (2017)

123. A Beast Well Tamed (The House of Jack the Ripper book 5) (2017)

124. Doctor Charles Grazier (The House of Jack the Ripper book 6) (2017)

125. The Raven Watcher (The House of Jack the Ripper book 7) (2017)

126. The Final Act (The House of Jack the Ripper book 8) (2017)

127. Stephen (2017)

128. The Spider (2017)

129. The Mermaid's Revenge (2017)

130. The Girl Who Threw Rocks at the Devil (2018)

131. Friend From the Internet (2018)

132. Beautiful Familiar (2018)

133. One Night at a Soul Auction (2018)

134. 16 Frames of the Devil's Face (2018)

135. The Haunting of Caldgrave House (2018)

136. Like Stones on a Crow's Back (The Deal Trilogy book 2) (2018)

137. Room 9 and Other Stories (2018)

138. The Gravest Girl of All (Grave Girl book 3) (2018)

139. Return to Thaxos (Dead Souls book 13) (2018)

140. The Madness of Annie Radford (The Asylum Trilogy book 3) (2018)

141. The Haunting of Briarwych Church (Briarwych book 1) (2018)

142. I Just Want You To Be Happy (2018)

143. Day 100 (Mass Extinction Event book 6) (2018)

144. The Horror of Briarwych Church (Briarwych book 2) (2018)

145. The Ghost of Briarwych Church (Briarwych book 3) (2018)

146. Lights Out (2019)

147. Apocalypse (The Ward Z Series book 3) (2019)

148. Days 101 to 108 (Mass Extinction Event book 7) (2019)

149. The Haunting of Daniel Bayliss (2019)

150. The Purchase (2019)

151. Harper's Hotel Ghost Girl (Death Herself book 4) (2019)

152. The Haunting of Aldburn House (2019)

153. Days 109 to 116 (Mass Extinction Event book 8) (2019)

154. Bad News (2019)

155. The Wedding of Rachel Blaine (2019)

156. Dark Little Wonders and Other Stories (2019)

157. The Music Man (2019)

158. The Vampire Falls (Three Nights of the Vampire book 1) (2019)

159. The Other Ann (2019)

160. The Butcher's Husband and Other Stories (2019)

161. The Haunting of Lannister Hall (2019)

162. The Vampire Burns (Three Nights of the Vampire book 2) (2019)

163. Days 195 to 202 (Mass Extinction Event book 9) (2019)

164. Escape From Hotel Necro (2019)

165. The Vampire Rises (Three Nights of the Vampire book 3) (2019)

166. Ten Chimes to Midnight: A Collection of Ghost Stories (2019)

167. The Strangler's Daughter (2019)

168. The Beast on the Tracks (2019)

169. The Haunting of the King's Head (2019)

170. I Married a Serial Killer (2019)

171. Your Inhuman Heart (2020)

172. Days 203 to 210 (Mass Extinction Event book 10) (2020)

173. The Ghosts of David Brook (2020)

174. Days 349 to 356 (Mass Extinction Event book 11) (2020)

175. The Horror at Criven Farm (2020)

176. Mary (2020)

177. The Middlewych Experiment (Chaos Gear Annie book 1) (2020)

178. Days 357 to 364 (Mass Extinction Event book 12) (2020)

179. Day 365: The Final Day (Mass Extinction Event book 13) (2020)

180. The Haunting of Hathaway House (2020)

181. Don't Let the Devil Know Your Name (2020)

182. The Legend of Rinth (2020)

183. The Ghost of Old Coal House (2020)

184. The Root (2020)

185. I'm Not a Zombie (2020)

186. The Ghost of Annie Close (2020)

187. The Disappearance of Lonnie James (2020)

188. The Curse of the Langfords (2020)

189. The Haunting of Nelson Street (The Ghosts of Crowford 1) (2020)

190. Strange Little Horrors and Other Stories (2020)

191. The House Where She Died (2020)

192. The Revenge of the Mercy Belle (The Ghosts of Crowford 2) (2020)

193. The Ghost of Crowford School (The Ghosts of Crowford book 3) (2020)

194. The Haunting of Hardlocke House (2020)

195. The Cemetery Ghost (2020)

196. You Should Have Seen Her (2020)

197. The Portrait of Sister Elsa (The Ghosts of Crowford book 4) (2021)

198. The House on Fisher Street (2021)

199. The Haunting of the Crowford Hoy (The Ghosts of Crowford 5) (2021)

200. Trill (2021)

201. The Horror of the Crowford Empire (The Ghosts of Crowford 6) (2021)

202. Out There (The Ted Armitage Trilogy book 1) (2021)

203. The Nightmare of Crowford Hospital (The Ghosts of Crowford 7) (2021)

204. Twist Valley (The Ted Armitage Trilogy book 2) (2021)

205. The Great Beyond (The Ted Armitage Trilogy book 3) (2021)

206. The Haunting of Edward House (2021)

207. The Curse of the Crowford Grand (The Ghosts of Crowford 8) (2021)

208. How to Make a Ghost (2021)

209. The Ghosts of Crossley Manor (The Ghosts of Crowford 9) (2021)

210. The Haunting of Matthew Thorne (2021)

211. The Siege of Crowford Castle (The Ghosts of Crowford 10) (2021)

212. Daisy: The Complete Series (2021)

213. Bait (Bait book 1) (2021)

214. Origin (Bait book 2) (2021)

215. Heretic (Bait book 3) (2021)

216. Anna's Sister (2021)

217. The Haunting of Quist House (The Rose Files 1) (2021)

218. The Haunting of Crowford Station (The Ghosts of Crowford 11) (2022)

219. The Curse of Rosie Stone (2022)

220. The First Order (The Chronicles of Sister June book 1) (2022)

221. The Second Veil (The Chronicles of Sister June book 2) (2022)

222. The Graves of Crowford Rise (The Ghosts of Crowford 12) (2022)

223. Dead Man: The Resurrection of Morton Kane (2022)

224. The Third Beast (The Chronicles of Sister June book 3) (2022)

225. The Legend of the Crossley Stag (The Ghosts of Crowford 13) (2022)

226. One Star (2022)

227. The Ghost in Room 119 (2022)

228. The Fourth Shadow (The Chronicles of Sister June book 4) (2022)

229. The Soldier Without a Past (Dead Souls book 14) (2022)

230. The Ghosts of Marsh House (2022)

231. Wax: The Complete Series (2022)

232. The Phantom of Crowford Theatre (The Ghosts of Crowford 14) (2022)

233. The Haunting of Hurst House (Mercy Willow book 1) (2022)

234. Blood Rains Down From the Sky (The Deal Trilogy book 3) (2022)

235. The Spirit on Sidle Street (Mercy Willow book 2) (2022)

236. The Ghost of Gower Grange (Mercy Willow book 3) (2022)

237. The Curse of Clute Cottage (Mercy Willow book 4) (2022)

238. The Haunting of Anna Jenkins (Mercy Willow book 5) (2023)

239. The Death of Mercy Willow (Mercy Willow book 6) (2023)

240. Angel (2023)

241. The Eyes of Maddy Park (2023)

242. If You Didn't Like Me Then, You Probably Won't Like Me Now (2023)

243. The Terror of Torfork Tower (Mercy Willow 7) (2023)

244. The Phantom of Payne Priory (Mercy Willow 8) (2023)

245. The Devil on Davis Drive (Mercy Willow 9) (2023)

246. The Haunting of the Ghost of Tom Bell (Mercy Willow 10) (2023)

247. The Other Ghost of Gower Grange (Mercy Willow 11) (2023)

248. The Haunting of Olive Atkins (Mercy Willow 12) (2023)

249. The End of Marcy Willow (Mercy Willow 13) (2023)

250. The Last Haunted House on Mars and Other Stories (2023)

251. 1689 (The Haunting of Hadlow House 1) (2023)

252. 1722 (The Haunting of Hadlow House 2) (2023)

253. 1775 (The Haunting of Hadlow House 3) (2023)

254. The Terror of Crowford Carnival (The Ghosts of Crowford 15) (2023)

255. 1800 (The Haunting of Hadlow House 4) (2023)

256. 1837 (The Haunting of Hadlow House 5) (2023)

257. 1885 (The Haunting of Hadlow House 6) (2023)

258. 1901 (The Haunting of Hadlow House 7) (2023)

259. 1918 (The Haunting of Hadlow House 8) (2023)

260. The Secret of Adam Grey (The Ghosts of Crowford 16) (2023)

261. 1926 (The Haunting of Hadlow House 9) (2023)

262. 1939 (The Haunting of Hadlow House 10) (2023)

263. The Fifth Tomb (The Chronicles of Sister June 5) (2023)
264. 1966 (The Haunting of Hadlow House 11) (2023)
265. 1999 (The Haunting of Hadlow House 12) (2023)
266. The Hauntings of Mia Rush (2023)
267. 2024 (The Haunting of Hadlow House 13) (2024)
268. The Sixth Window (The Chronicles of Sister June 6) (2024)
269. Little Miss Dead (The Horrors of Sobolton 1) (2024)
270. Swan Territory (The Horrors of Sobolton 2) (2024)
271. Dead Widow Road (The Horrors of Sobolton 3) (2024)
272. The Haunting of Stryke Brothers (The Ghosts of Crowford 17) (2024)
273. In a Lonely Grave (The Horrors of Sobolton 4) (2024)
274. Electrification (The Horrors of Sobolton 5) (2024)
275. Man on the Moon (The Horrors of Sobolton 6) (2024)

AMY CROSS

For more information, visit:

www.amycross.com

AMY CROSS

Printed in Great Britain
by Amazon